MW00534039

DANCE WITH MY FATHER

SABIN PRENTIS

This is a work of fiction. All names, characters, places, and incidents are the product of the author's imagination. Any resemblance to real events or persons, living or dead, is entirely coincidental.

Copyright © 2022 by Sabin Prentis Duncan

Published by Fielding Books, Richmond, VA

Cover Model: Bishop M. Louis Lacey

Photography by Franklin Fitzgerald

ISBN: 978-0-9984885-8-5

For my late dad, Fred L. Duncan, Jr.
and my late father-in-law, John L. Cox, Jr.
You set the bar really high and one of my life's greatest joys is
becoming the father you showed me how to be.

Damon, Joanne, Fred & Sabin - 2013

AUTHOR'S NOTE

Dance With My Father is the concluding novel of
the **Love & Family Trilogy** that includes
Compared To What and *Better Left Unsaid*.

Hopefully, you will choose to enjoy them all.

Thank you for your support.

Much love,
Sabin Prentis

"A truly rich man is one whose children run into his arms when his hands are empty."

— UNKNOWN

STRANGE FRUIT
Billie Holiday

1951
Florida

Of all the horrific details exposed on the scorched and mutilated corpse that dangled from the seared and frayed rope, Cleveland's tear-filled eyes fixed upon his father's feet. A soul-shaking fright consumed him when he recognized the remaining charred numbs that had been his father's toes and his horror was heightened by what he did not see.

The evil act that snuffed out his father's life also robbed him of his work boots.

Cleveland could not recall a time outside their home, when his father was not wearing his over-worn, multi-creased, tattered-leather work boots.

Granted, four-year-olds do not hold large repositories of memories, but for young Cleveland Robeson, the essence of his father was contained in his weathered boots.

Cleveland and his twin, Columbus, would tug and pull at those boots when helping their dad after an arduous day in the pecan grove. For the twins, pulling off their dad's boots earned them an affectionate head rub from their father's ruggedly calloused hands.

Willie Robeson was a man of few words. His entire life was spent within three different sharecropping plantations in Baker County. Among the other pecan-pickers, he was the sole reader. His reading of outdated copies of the Baltimore Afro-American and other Negro newspapers to his fellow sharecroppers roused the ire of the locals. Negro newspapers were contraband, and reading them was akin to a felony. Some Baker County natives were inhospitable to news about Jackie Robinson, Ralph Bunche, or the NAACP. To them, Willie's reading of these assumed illegal papers aloud proved that he was an uppity-Negro exposing forbidden taboo.

To the pecan-pickers, Willie's narrations parceled out modicums of hope and a foreignly fantastic vision of a world beyond the groves. A vision that also fueled Willie's desires for his twin boys. While he had read about far-away places where Negroes could earn a fair wage, those particles of possibility seemed impossibly beyond his grasp. Nevertheless, each night after his boys tussled with his work boots, he would lift them into his lap and stare into their eyes as if telepathy could convey that there is more to life than pecan groves.

Willie's wife had some experiences outside the pecan groves which included having taken a few classes at Edward Waters College. With her education, she taught her husband to read. Her periodic sojourns into Jacksonville also provided access to newspapers and a worldview beyond the county. It also gave her the certainty of expedience following their sorrowful benediction with Willie's charred corpse.

Josephine had as many possessions as she could carry bundled onto her back. Columbus squeezed her left thigh and buried his face into her hip. Cleveland held her right hand and several moments after her pain-stricken, heartbro-ken, sobbing rhetorical question, "Willie, what have they done to you?" Cleveland asked a question of his own, "Mama, where Papa's boots?"

February 2, 2015

The weather reports predicted heavy snow. All of the schools and the majority of businesses had closed for the day. Except for Supportive Hugs Counseling Center which was led by its founder, Dr. Linda Daniels.

One of Cleveland's deliberate acts of affection for his wife following the death of her close friend was the coercion to see a therapist. It did not take long for Elaine Robeson and Dr. Daniels to establish a rapport mirroring one of old friends rather than that of a patient and therapist. During previous sessions, Dr. Daniels asked Elaine to invite Cleve to join them. Each time he finagled a way out of the meeting.

However this morning the snow deterred Cleve's usual retreat to the coffee shop.

Additionally, all of Dr. Daniels' appointments canceled excepted Elaine. Because of the weather, Cleve drove her to therapy in his work van because he wanted to assure her safe arrival. After arriving to Dr. Daniels' office in Detroit's New Center Area, the ladies invited him inside so that he would not have to wait outside in the cold. Minutes later, he was on the couch next to Elaine. An hour later, he was recalling the graphic particulars of his father's murder.

Despite their nearly fifty years of marriage, Elaine only knew that Cleve's father died when he was young. At times, she thought him evasive when recalling his childhood. Considering the nomadic loneliness of her own childhood, there was a part of her heart that understood not wanting to rehash the past. Over time, she learned to leave well enough alone. Though this morning, she realized had she learned of the details, she would not have been prepared to console her husband.

The session started innocently. Cleve assumed that talks about grieving were related to Elaine's healing from Francine's suicide. However, Dr. Daniels was steering the conversation toward healing and reinvention following the death of a loved one. She was an accomplished and compassionate therapist who could frame questions in such a way that a patient's deepest secrets would be unearthed.

Cleve had been saddled with the trauma of his father's murder for over half a century and as Elaine watched, it appeared that a half a century worth of tears streaked down his face.

After the hugs, back rubs, and three boxes of Kleenex, a few things became clear: work boots equalled provision and security. Which indirectly explained Cleve's attachment to what he called "broken-in" boots, including the ones he was wearing. Which in his own self-image, Cleveland saw himself as the husband his mother needed and the father for which he and his brother longed.

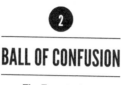

BALL OF CONFUSION
The Temptations

February 2, 2015

The school closings provided ample opportunity for another meeting, one which would prove to be quite detrimental to the existence of Detroit Public Schools. This meeting, led by the state-appointed Emergency Manager, was an early step in an accelerated succession plan.

Citing health challenges and concealing his premonitions that this state-directed takeover of DPS would ultimately fail, the Emergency Manager shared with his executive cabinet his intention to resign from the post. He also shared, in guarded and measured words, that he had consulted with the governor and other stakeholders in Lansing, and that they felt that an interim emergency manager should finish the school year. There was no discussion of the replacement process. Those people, decision-makers, and individuals far removed from the lives of everyday Detroiters quickly endorsed the Executive Assistant for the interim role.

The Executive Assistant?

Not the former school superintendent. Not the recently

promoted district superintendent. Not the former teacher of the year, nor the retired curriculum specialist—the people in power were in favor of Wellington Shelby taking the mantle of leadership during the school district's season of tumult.

When the Emergency Manager shared the announcement with his cabinet, the disappointment and disbelief from the others coalesced into a chest-expanding, unfunded surge of confidence within Wellington. Within seconds, he was imagining a Napoleonic vision of how he would transform DPS. He figured that his dearth of experience was an asset because Detroit was in the shape it was in because of the experienced people, right?

"Hell nawl!" Protested the Curriculum Specialist. "Since when does managing social media equal leadership?"

The former school superintendent added, "All of our progress will halted."

The district superintendent, the one most Detroiters assumed was the heir apparent and in most cases, who many believed was the last hope for resurrection, was speechlessly confused. A confusion in whose silence, Shelby tweeted to the district's official Twitter account:

I'm so proud of our hard work for Detroit's children. Things are getting better. #changeisgood #DPS4life

The tweet was accompanied by a selfie picture that featured the strikingly handsome Shelby in the forefront and a perplexed executive cabinet in the background.

"Put that damn phone away!" shouted the Curriculum Specialist, whose shock at the announcement was another gasoline-soaked log on her burning disdain for Shelby.

"Mr. Shelby, we need you to focus on today's agenda," was the Emergency Manager's effort to reel Wellington's attention back to the meeting. He had hired Shelby because of his age and the hope that his social media prowess could lead to the "re-telling" of the DPS story without the negative media slant employed by the local newspaper. However, a recent review of the district's Instagram page displayed that within the last twenty posts, Mr. Shelby was prominently featured in fourteen of them. Additionally, the agreed-upon use of Twitter to share insider facts about increased reading performance or spotlight effective teachers has been transformed into Wellington's spin on district matters. The emergency manager had planned to discuss these matters with Shelby, but now recognized he had waited too long. In a flash of prescience, he knew that this failed revolution would not be televised; it would be tweeted.

Technically, Wellington Shelby was not a member of the executive cabinet, yet people had come to accept his proximity to the Emergency Manager in a gopher-director relationship, sort of a Wellington-as-Jerome to the Emergency Manager's Morris Day. The difference is that Jerome knows he is not Morris, while Wellington believes he can lead The Time or the school district.

Moreover, with the backing of the colonialists state-level overseers, he was empowered to expedite the demise of a community—a notion that would become obvious to all, except Wellington Shelby.

3

YOU'VE GOT A FRIEND

Donny Hathaway

February 2, 2015

L ike synchronized singers, when Songhai and Stokely saw each other, they would melodically murmur each other's names. "Stok-leeeeee," Songhai would coo to her baby brother as she opened her arms. "SSSoooooooonnnggg," Stokely would say in return as he would meet her embrace. Even as adults, they would playfully hug each other just as they had as kids.

Song's nearly twenty year prison stint had almost wiped away the practice, yet in the weeks following her release, the affectionate greeting returned.

"How's it going with you and dad?" Stokely inquired about his sister's role in their father's plumbing business. Stokely knew that business had prospered with the addition of Songhai's organization of scheduling and equipment, yet he still wanted to hear his sister's take.

"Did you know Dad had all his contacts on scraps of torn paper, napkins, and the backs of business cards?" Song asked in astonishment before adding, "He was handwriting receipts on notebook paper!" They laughed in unison, as they knew their father's expertise in plumbing did not carry over into the management of his business. Their love for Cleve came with an acceptance of his duct-taped flip phone and other out-dated modes of operation.

Song continued, "That's why you're here."

Stokley was confused.

"You are going to show me how to set up a website for the business," Song said, with that declarative tone their mother used.

With the instant clarity of a turned-on lightbulb, Stokely recognized the wisdom in his sister's strategy. He smiled and replied, "Let's do it."

August 1962

The Contours were inquisitively wailing from the radio speakers, wanting to know if the young lady loved them now that they could dance as a semi-permanent cloud of cigarette smoke lingered near the ceiling. The fan that blew from the corner provided little relief in the small sweatbox of a billiard parlor, known as Mr. B's.

The billiard parlor was located on Trumbull Avenue, a few blocks from the Jeffries Homes. Mr. B's was a haven for small-time pimps, aspiring hustlers, and old heads who frequented it out of habit. It was also where Cleveland manned the shoe shine stand and Columbus refined his cue stick skills.

Occasionally, Columbus would shine shoes with his brother, but those occasions were far and few between. They intentionally divided their energies as a means to maximize their earnings. One strategy was for Cleveland to talk to any new customer about the kid over at table three who was losing all his money while talking big. Typically, by the time

Cleveland laid it on thick enough, the newcomer with freshly shined shoes would take the bait and figure he could beat Columbus in a quick game. All the real players knew Columbus and recognized his hustle, which meant that the next time he shot after intentionally scratching, he was going to run the rest of the table.

On this particular day, a fast-talking con man from the Eastside took Cleveland's bait. He sized up Columbus and guessed the game. He played it sheepishly with a small bet and peeped the hustle. His double or nothing hustle was only one step up on the con game pyramid, yet he was still besting Columbus that afternoon.

Until Cleveland, who was aware of the ass-whipping his brother was taking, did a little something extra with the shoe-shining. Regulars knew the popping of Cleveland's towel meant he had just finished a job. The sound of the popping towel was as normal as the radio noise. However, right at the moment that The Contours were going to ask whether the lady liked the Mashed Potato or the Twist, Cleveland flung his towel with additional emphasis, and as it reverberated from the "pop," it hit the East-sider in the back of his head. Just enough of a distraction to mess up his shot. Columbus recovered and won the game. When the East-sider revealed his switchblade, Mr. B brandished his .38 and sort of held the man hostage while telling Cleveland and Columbus to get on home. They would return the next day, and the routine would resume, minus the East-sider.

I SAY A LITTLE PRAYER

Aretha Franklin

February 5, 2015

Stokely and Phoenix had the damnedest time leaving the apartment in a timely manner. They were both responsible and punctual. However, a delayed departure always resulted from their still-on-a-honeymoon lovebird morning affections. Kisses on the neck while the other brushes their teeth. A little extra umph with the lotion as one moisturizes the other after a shower. An unexpected hug and blushing glances in the mirror after Stokely zips Phoenix's dress and then wraps his arms around her. Phoenix's damnnear maternal inquires about Stokely's plans for the day and whether he has all he needs. Seriously, they will be back together in a handful of hours, but to hear Phoenix communicate during their morning good-byes, one would assume Stokely was Abubakari, setting off across the seas.

After they shared a good-bye kiss next to Phoenix's Jeep, she said, "Stokely, did you know that I pray for you?"

Stokely looked puzzled and attempted humor, "I knew there was a little church girl inside of you." Phoenix returned a chuckle and followed with, "No, but seriously. Sometimes I pray for your strength. Sometimes clarity, sometimes... well, I don't know. I just know you're with me even when you aren't there."

Stokely really did not know what to say. He thought, "Oh, I pray for you too," would sound disingenuous. Indeed, he thought of Phoenix frequently, but praying for her was not how he would describe it. Instead, he leaned in for another kiss and whispered, "No wonder things are going so well." It was Phoenix's turn to be puzzled. To which Stokely responded, "You know what they say about the prayers of the righteous..." They giggled and kissed again. Unbeknownst to Stokely, he was going to need those prayers.

WHEN EDNA TOLD HIM THERE WAS A GUEST IN HIS OFFICE, Stokely assumed it was a representative from the accounting firm whose proposal he had finished reviewing. He rushed into his office without giving Edna a chance to finish. The suddenness with which he lost his breath was as audible as a great sucking of wind.

When he flung open the door, the trajectory of his vision first caught her stylishly elaborate high-heeled boots. Boots that certainly made her stand at least 6'3." She wore a pants suit, yet the contours of her thighs and hips made themselves known underneath the fashionably tailored wool. Stokely knew instantly that this was not the accounting firm representative, and in the nano-seconds it took for his eyes to travel up her body, the flashbacks of the good times they shared flickered like a sentimental montage across his mind.

"Do you always burst into your office this way?" Tanya asked.

Her locs were in a type of up-do that could easily be described as a crown. Furthermore, the year since their breakup had done nothing to diminish her sultry confidence or striking beauty. From the first time he saw her, throughout their relationship, and now, at this moment, Tanya maintained a stunning, punch-in-mouth-speechless-ness, type of beauty.

Stokely did an awkward sigh-laugh as she stepped across the office and gave him a friendly, side-shoulder, professional embrace.

"It's good to see you, Stokely," she said with honest friendliness.

"Yeah, it's good to see you too, Tanya," he replied with a comparable friendliness that covered his what-is-she-doing-here surprise.

"I had almost forgotten how handsome you are," she said playfully, releasing herself from the hug. Stokely was afraid to return the compliment, fearing that any talk of Tanya's beauty would send him down a rabbit hole of emotionality. With as much caution as he could muster, he answered, "Thanks Tanya. It's nice to see that you've still got your head-turning magic." Even as he said the words, he wished he could take them back as she smiled and did a slow, seductive 360 degree turn so that he could see all of her.

"Do you like my boots?"

"They are nice. Where did you get them? They don't seem like something you would find in Nashville."

"Don't sleep on Nashville," she playfully warned, while adding, "But no, Oscar got them for me last time we were in New York." She pulled up her pants leg so that Stokely could admire their design or the way they hugged her calf.

"You came to show me your boots?"

Tanya laughed, "I see you still have your sense of humor."

Stokely sat at his desk as she pulled up a chair. With a steady gradualness, like an ice cube becoming one with a pot of boiling water, her flirtatiousness was replaced by a scared solemness.

"Stokely ..." she sighed deeply, "Oscar is dying."

The silence circumnavigated around them like an eagle in the sky before he strikes his prey. Much like the suddenness of the eagle's strike, Tanya added, "And I think it's worthwhile if he and Phoenix get a chance to talk." She paused and took a deep breath, as if trying to call back the tears that were starting to form. "Who knows? Maybe they could clear the air. You know, both of them. Maybe they could get some... " Her words trailed off as she looked at the floor. "I don't know about her, but maybe Oscar, maybe he can gain some peace."

The end of Stokely's affair with Tanya was devastating. While the meeting and courting of Phoenix had redemptive attributes, it was also a sincerely promising relationship. At the moment Tanya spoke of bringing Oscar and Phoenix together, all Stokely could imagine was what happened the last time they were all together. He was saddened by the memory of Oscar leaving in an ambulance and horrified by the thought of Phoenix disappearing from his life. This confluence of confusion formed on his tongue.

"Tanya, I... I don't know what to say.' He bit his top lip. "I mean, yeah, peace is important, and I guess for a..." he didn't want to say it, so he kind of whispered it, "A dying man..." Regret flooded him. "I just... I'll... I will talk to Phoenix."

Tanya reached across the desk and clasped his hands. She had begun crying, and with tears slowly oozing down her face, she mouthed, "Thank you."

5

STUBBORN KIND OF FELLOW

Marvin Gaye

February 6, 2015

"I ain't going," Phoenix said in a huff.

Denise, her mother, exhaled a long sigh before speaking just above a whisper, "Phoenix, honey, you really should reconsider your position." This was one of those times when parents who have raised their daughters to be independent thinkers dread. They understand the daughter's position while also having the benefit of life experience to know that the daughter's position is short-sighted. It's a delicate place because the parents do not want to usurp their daughter's spirit, yet they are conflicted because once she proceeds down one path after this fork in the road, there is no opportunity for a do-over.

"Level with me—what is the reason why you don't want to see your father? Hopefully, it's not the way you received the news," Denise said, to indirectly acknowledge the unusual way in which Phoenix learned of her father's condition.

Phoenix exhaled a large "whew" while shaking her head with eyes open wide. "Ma, that's a whole 'nuther thing in and of itself." She shook her head some more and added a rhetorical question, "Seeing my father means spending time with my man's ex-girlfriend?" Her disbelieving incredulity was captured in her raised shoulders and palms-up gesture.

"Yeah, that's definitely something, no doubt about it," Denise responded, after a sip of wine. She paused for a moment before adding, "To anyone else, though, that sounds like drama; but you? You know, Stokely." Denise chuckled as she continued, "I mean, as much as you are all over each other, you would know if there was any left over longing." She sipped again. "And you would certainly recognize it if he were keeping secrets or avoiding anything."

Phoenix accepted this truth with a smile to acknowledge her mother's teasing. "When he first told me about her, I felt like he was in some type of shock over their break-up..." Before Phoenix could finish, Denise inserted, "But she was, I mean, is married."

"Right, he said that up front. But after we started seeing each other again, I would ask him directly and indirectly, and I am convinced he moved on." Phoenix nodded her head in acknowledgement. "Their relationship is over."

With both hands clasping the chalice, Denise leaned forward and pointed an accusatory finger, "So the discomforting thoughts or stories you've made up in your mind about Stokely and Oscar's wife are really a smokescreen of avoidance for you taking initiative to see your father."

There was silence as Phoenix grabbed a pillow and pulled her knees to her chest on the loveseat opposite her mother. She grimaced both painfully and childishly as she responded, "Dang Ma, you didn't have to put it like that."

Denise leaned back in her chair and snickered, "Well, we got that truth out in the open." The rim of the wine glass did not conceal her accusatory glare as she sipped.

February 6, 2015
Nashville

"I ain't going," Oscar said, after a fit of coughing.

Tanya brought her palms together in a praying steeple in front of her face. For a second, she pondered the burden of watching her husband die. Then she thought of the hopelessness of these doctor visits, which had taken on the feeling of a countdown. She totally understood why Oscar did not want to be reminded of his mortality. As if the bedpan, soiled sheets, over-sized and ill-fitting pajamas, and night stand full of pills weren't enough of a reminder, hobbling through the doctor's office with everyone looking at him in pity could easily be the straw that would break a camel's back.

But what was she supposed to do?

Yes, home health aides do the technical medical care, but Tanya watches them like a suspicious overseer. Despite taking a leave from her job, tending to Oscar's comfort and the remote chance for recovery was more taxing than she would ever admit. At various points in her life, her ability to be decisive and to draw a line in the sand to move on has served her well. All of the ailments and treatments say one thing about Oscar's health predicament, but what else can she do? Tanya is a doer. She makes things happen. This afternoon, she understands that she has to make this doctor's visit happen despite its futility because she would not be able to live with herself knowing she was passively idle during Oscar's time of need.

She extended her arm and grasped Oscar's armpit, and with her other arm, she reached around his back. He met her slight pull with a rising effort that resulted in him sitting up on the edge of the bed. She kissed him on the forehead and pointed to the clock.

"One hour from now, we could be enjoying your favorite

gourmet mint ginger sherbet. But the only way we can do that is if we get to this appointment," she said as she looked him in the eye.

His stubbornness melted under her gaze, and he slowly flung his legs over the edge of the mattress. Jokingly, he added, "You're always so damn compelling."

They both laughed with sad chuckles of acceptance.

6

TALKIN' LOUD AND SAYING NOTHIN'

James Brown

February 9, 2015

Whoever planned the Meet-the-Manager community session that would introduce Wellington Shelby as the Interim Emergency Manager for Detroit Public Schools should have done so with their resignation attached to the agenda because the event was worse than a fiasco; it would nearly become a burning at the stake.

The miscalculation began with the choice to not have the retiring emergency manager present. Despite the discord he caused, his authoritarian, paternal, tough-love presence permitted just enough consideration for an audience to grant a benefit-of-the-doubt preliminary listen. His announcement style was direct: "This is the challenge, and this is what I propose we do." He was calm and concise.

Concision was not only one of Shelby's weaknesses; it was not even on his radar of values. Perhaps his high opinion of himself misled him to believe that everyone adored him in a similar way. His propensity for hyperbole and his I'm-the-savior-you've-been-waiting-for perspective made him a bloody carcass in the shark-infested seas of festering parental discontent.

But no one would have been able to convince him otherwise. He took the podium in front of a congregation of blue-collar, working poor, and frustrated parents, along with a sprinkling of some obligatory rabble rousers, in some Italian loafers, without socks (during February in Detroit!), a slim-cut (read: tight-fitting) tailored three-piece suit, with bedazzling cufflinks that dinged the podium with a soft treble that offset the heavy thud his titanium Hublot watch made, along with a colorful peacock bouffant bow tie, with a matching pocket kerchief, some of that fill-in spray along his hairline to make it more pronounced, and enough cologne to rival a Parisian boudoir. Any accusations of cockiness and tone-deafness would have been far too modest.

For a moment, the audience stared at him. It seemed they had seen him before, yet right now, he appeared to be an apparition from the land of delusional self-assuredness.

WELLINGTON BEGAN, "GOOD MORNING, I AM YOUR NEWLY appointed Interim Emergency Manager and I stand before you today to seize the reins of our educational system and steer it triumphantly toward the finish line of high achievement and scholarship." The pronouncement caused waves of confusion to ripple through the audience. Not only was the audience taken aback by the declaration, his proper diction reinforced the concern of whether he knew who he was talking to and whether he could speak for them.

Wellington extended his hands outward toward the crowd comparable to Dr. Martin Luther King, Jr. at the March on Washington and channeled a thunderous urgency in his voice that would impress T.D. Jakes, "For too long, our children have been overlooked, cast aside, and led astray! But today," he knocked on the wood podium twice and continued, "Today is a new day. The starting point for an ascendancy of accountability and the decline of ineptitude is now, for I will blaze a path toward a transformation of this school district and the betterment of our community!"

Confusion had given way to befuddlement. As the audience looked to each other for understanding, Cora Neighbors tapped the microphone in the aisle intended for the question and answer period. She had heard enough and could not hold her question any longer.

"Excuse me, Mr. Manager. Some of us been wondering just how closing twenty schools is gonna, well, you know, uh, whatcha say—yeah, be to the 'betterment of our community.'"

"Who said we are closing twenty schools?" Shelby responded in shock.

"Y'all did, right on page thirty-seven of the Revitalization Plan. The fourteenth bullet under the Solutions for Solvency section - you read it, right?" Mrs. Neighbors asked sincerely.

Shelby's apparent confusion told Detroiters what they needed to know.

Mr. Jefferson, a long time custodian with the district and former representative to the recently-abolished union, shouted, "He ain't read shit!" A declaration that prompted within Shelby a slow-moving slideshow of his childhood and subsequent years. He looked around the audience as the escalating anger prompted him to fear for his life.

Someone else shouted, "This is some BULLshit!"

Rancor simmered and profanity flew freely.

"Aw hell, nawl!"

"What the fuck is this shit?"

"Is it about you or the kids?"

"Is this some kind of joke?"

Then Shelby committed a cardinal sin. In a vain effort to

regain control, he said, "You people ... " and before he could finish the sentence, the crowd erupted in boos, hisses, and vociferous shouts of anger.

Stepping in from the sidelines toward the podium was the Reverend Amos Thigpen. He patted Shelby on the back and gestured toward the microphone as if asking, "May I?"

Wellington Shelby was so shaken that he nodded a hurried yes.

Initially, Thigpen hummed into the mic—reminiscent of the opening bars of the outro verse from the TV show, *Good Times*. Slowly, the volume of anger diminished.

Then he whispered, "Detroit?" and the volume was quelled a bit more. "Detroit, my home. My people, Detroit," then he hummed a little more before raising his voice to a conversational tone. "Oh Detroit, we've been through so much." An audience member shouted, "Too much!" From which Thigpen took the baton and said, "That's right, sister. Too much... to turn back now." A few people clapped, but most appeared to be catching their breath, as if counting to ten after losing their temper.

"Too much, I tell you, to turn back now." He paused for effect and gave Shelby a look that said, "Step back and watch how it's done." Shelby stepped aside, and Thigpen unholstered the microphone, whipped the cord around from the podium, and proceeded into the audience. When he reached the fourth row, he did a whipping turn and pointed to Shelby in a manner that would have made the Jackson 5 proud.

"Mr. Shelby is here to carry out the state's effort to right the mighty ship of DPS. But to me, Mr. Shelby isn't some stooge of the state, " To which an audience member asked, "Well, what is he?" Thigpen grinned a sinister smile and charmingly shared, "He is our brother, and he is willing to work with us, receive our input, and take the necessary steps for us to regain control of our school system." He paused again, looking around at the crowd, before fixing his gaze upon Shelby, "Isn't that right, Brother Shelby?"

Shelby said an unconvincing, "Yes."

"Can you say it a little louder for the people in the back? You are here to help us regain control of OUR school system. Right, Brother Shelby?"

"Yes, that is..."

Thigpen cut him off and turned to the crowd. "We are going to hold Brother Shelby accountable for his promise, his purpose, and his word to the students, teachers, and families of Detroit. We are not going to allow those fancy suits in Lansing to lead our brother down the pilfering path of exploitation, are we?"

Surprisingly, a handful of people shouted, "Hell no!"

"Saints, I mean Detroit..." Before proceeding, Thigpen let a little mischievous chuckle escape before adding, "Brother Shelby will need an accountability partner." He nodded his head as he looked around the audience. "Someone that will keep him focused on our goal."

A woman shouted, "I know that's right!"

"Someone who will keep his feet to the fire should those fancy suits distract him."

A raspy-voiced man shouted, "You preaching now!"

Thigpen re-approached the podium, extended his hand to Shelby, who grasped it and was snatched into Thigpen's embrace. "Detroit, I will work alongside Brother Shelby and see to it that our children and our schools get the service we deserve!"

Members of the crowd stood to applaud as Thigpen held up both their hands in triumph and walked away from the podium.

Shelby murmured, "Thank you," to which Thigpen retorted, through clenched teeth and holding a phony smile, "Thank me later. We've got work to do."

7

THE HIGHWAYS OF MY LIFE

The Isley Brothers

February 9, 2015

I t was not rooted in anger, yet for Stokely, Phoenix's silence was troubling.

He had been driving just over three hours, and they were passing through downtown Dayton, Ohio, en route to Nashville. Stokely attempted to break the silence and off-handedly commented, "If you take that highway right there, you'd be on your way to Wilberforce."

Phoenix accepted his olive branch of conversation with a question, "How many times have you been that way?"

It appeared as if Stokely was counting all the trips in his head before giving up and saying, "I really don't think it's an exaggeration to say at least forty times." Phoenix's little smile gave him permission to continue.

"What's funny is Wilberforce doesn't even have a football team, but they still have Homecoming! And that joint be off the hook!" They laughed together at the irony before Stokely continued. "In the dictionary, right next to 'Engaged Alumni' is a picture of my mom." They chuckled some more. "Like, she took us to Wilberforce's Homecoming, sometimes to Central State's Homecoming, a couple of graduations, and other events." Stokely added with extra emphasis, "She has been making monthly donations to the WU for as long as I can remember." He pondered a second before adding, "Shot, probably since the 70s. Her love for Wilberforce is serious!"

It wasn't long before they were proceeding out of Dayton, but the reflective conversation continued. "When I was about eight, my dad told me that I was taking over as the man on the trip because he had been on one trip too many. After he passed the mantle, he rarely went, but my mom had her girl-friends and me and Song clad in all that green and gold as we made the trip without him."

The silence returned as Stokely kicked himself internally after recognizing he was discussing his father and the purpose of their trip was a fragile attempt for Phoenix to reconcile with her father. He did not want to trigger comparisons or conjure the void Phoenix felt growing up without her dad. So he shut up. Well, at least for a few minutes. Around the time they neared Cincinnati, Phoenix reached inside her large purse and withdrew a Ziploc bag of snacks she had prepared for the journey. Her purse contained eight of these bags, with additional snacks packed in the luggage in the bed of Stokely's truck.

She popped a small fistful of trail mix in her mouth before gesturing the open bag toward Stokely as if asking, "Do you want some?" Stokely reached for some and glanced down and caught a glimpse of a number of similarly packed snack bags in her purse on the floor board. He then looked at the road ahead before turning to Phoenix and asking, "Do you think we'll have enough snacks to make it?" There was a split second of silence before they both erupted in laughter.

May 1972

Cleve stole a glance over at his wife, Elaine, whose head was resting against the window of his Camaro as he proceeded down I75 towards Cincinnati. She was exhausted as the day had been an emotional rollercoaster.

The day began with her graduation from Wilberforce—a euphoric moment shared with her best friends, Joyce and Francine. Both Joyce and Francine were congratulated by their extended network of family and friends, but for Elaine, there was only one celebrant to cheer her on: the sole person who makes up her real family, her husband, Cleveland.

Growing up, she was shuffled from one relative's house to the next. Frequently, she heard, "This is what family is for," while sensing unenthused and begrudging duty beneath the words. She was born to a teenaged mother who had been sent north to have the baby she conceived out of wedlock. Days after Elaine's birth, her mother returned to Arkansas without her. Over time, her mother's occasional visits became irregular, and the two weeks Elaine stayed in Arkansas when she was sixteen only made her feel like more of an afterthought. Although life had cultivated a fierce independence within her, she longed for the comfort of family.

After learning that none of the relatives with whom she had lived while growing up would be able to attend the ceremony, Elaine got the fantastical idea of visiting her parents to show them her degree. She would not readily admit it, but she also wanted to show them she made it without their help. She imagined that her mother would understand, but her father, whom she had never met, probably would not grasp what her graduation meant to her in spite of his lack of contribution. There was an even sadder chance that he may not even care.

When he saw his wife sleeping, Cleve felt a strong sense

of protectiveness. Growing up, he imagined that he would be as good of a husband as he fantasized that his father was, and since their courthouse wedding last December, he believed he had been. But Elaine was not some prop in an ego-filling production of an idealized life; she was his sincere soulmate, and the life they were creating was far better than any of his dreams. The opportunity to meet her parents was one that he undertook in full anticipation of the need to be supportive in preparation for whatever disappointments may lay ahead. Although he was uneasy about this trip, he knew it was necessary. And while he did not know exactly what he would do should things go awry, he was prepared for the worst, even as he hoped for the best.

8

BE TRUE TO THE GAME

Ice Cube

February 10, 2015

The meeting with the parents rattled Wellington Shelby. He could not wrap his mind around why the community did not recognize him as the panacea for the problems facing the school district. If the old administration or even the previous emergency manager could have gotten the job done, then the governor would not have needed to select him. But the fact remains that the governor did select him, which was coupled with another fact that would evade Wellington's thinking, that he was a pawn in a larger scheme of interference.

On a morning when he should have been meeting with his administrative cabinet, Wellington postponed that meeting for later. There was an impromptu meeting that required his attention, one with Pastor Thigpen.

When Wellington walked through the church doors, he was greeted by Thigpen, who placed a hand on each of Wellington's shoulders and said, "Brother Shelby, I am so glad that you could meet on such short notice." Thigpen pursed his lips and dipped his head in a manner to establish eye contact with the uncomfortable Shelby.

He continued, "After those people misunderstood you, I went home and prayed to the Lord for guidance. I prayed for your strength and I prayed that the Lord would use me as a crutch of support when you face tough times. Each time Thigpen said, "The Lord," he shook Shelby's shoulders. "I tarried for hours, hoping the Lord would send me a sign. Send me a dove after the flood. Send us a ram in the bush."

"I wept and read my Bible while waiting on the Lord's sign." Thigpen inhaled a deep breath, expanded his flabby chest to its fullest capacity, and smiled a knowing smile. "But oh my Lord, late in the midnight hour, revealed to me Brother Shelby, a little something you should do." This got Shelby's full attention, even as Thigpen continued to hold his shoulders.

"The Lord laid on my heart," Thigpen momentarily removed his right hand and placed it over his heart. Once he returned it to Shelby's shoulder, he continued, "The Lord told me to tell you to focus on minority contracts."

Wellington was confused. Which was the opening Thigpen needed. He draped one arm around Wellington's shoulder and turned him back to the door. "You see son, these people don't know you." Thigpen stepped back and did an up and down motion with his hand, "They see these fancy clothes." Thigpen then pointed outside to Shelby's Lexus coupe parked behind his late model, vinyl-roofed Cadillac. "They see that fancy Japanese car." Then he leaned closer and sniffed the air around Shelby, "And they smell this fancy cologne and they figure you can't speak for us."

Welligton's brow furrowed. Thigpen poked him in the chest, "But I know your heart. The Lord showed me your good intent." He paused to let the idea sink in before continuing, "See these people need something to believe in, something to hold onto. So this is what you do, you say you looked at the contracts approved by the last Emergency Manager and say the diversity of the companies that were awarded contracts does not match the diversity of our city. Then with the absolute power you have, cancel those contracts and award them to some minorities."

Thigpen could see that his words were penetrating Shelby's thinking. He drove the point home further. "It doesn't even matter who the new companies are, just parade some black faces, and make sure a couple of them are women-folk, maybe even a Mexican, but get those new contracts awarded and them contractors in the schools before the end of next week. The people will be impressed, and it will give us time to advance our real agenda."

A few moments of silence passed before Shelby said, "Thank you, Pastor. I'm going to get on that today." With phony modesty, Thigpen patted his back, "Oh son, don't thank me, thank the Lord. He can make a way even when we don't see one." He held open the door as Shelby exited, "Let's touch base tomorrow afternoon to see how you've progressed."

Before starting his car, Shelby sent a tweet:

DPS' renaissance is for real. Details coming soon. #DPS4life #renaissance

9

JUST THE TWO OF US

Grover Washington, Jr. & Bill Withers

February 10, 2015

When Stokely told Cleve he was driving Phoenix to see her dying father, Cleve assured his son this would be the most challenging moment of their relationship so far. With that announcement, Stokely took a seat at his parents' kitchen table as a means of gathering some equilibrium.

Elaine walked in as he sat. "Hey baby, how are you..." She looked to Cleve, whose expression conveyed that he had things under control. Cleve said, "Yeah, Stokely and Phoenix 'bout to head on down to Nashville to see her old boy."

Elaine froze. She was aware of what happened last time the couple met with Phoenix's dad and his wife. At that moment, the words, "Why are they..." took form on Elaine's tongue. Cleve interjected, "Seems like he is in tough shape and they ain't too sure if he's going to make it."

Elaine looked at Cleve, who nodded a slow "Yes," and then looked at her son. She placed a hand on his cheek and said, "Well, I'm gonna go on ahead and let y'all work this out." This time, Cleve nodded a more assured "Yes," and as she passed to leave the room, he did a soft grip on her behind. She playfully swatted at his hand and told him, "You need to focus on that man's business that y'all need to handle." Then she winked, "Me and you can handle our business later."

Cleve smiled a bit before turning to his son, who was trying to suppress an embarrassed chuckle. "Look here Stokely, you handle this trip right and you'll be able to grab ass, too. But right now, you need to focus on the next few days."

Cleve pulled a chair, spun it around, sat, and folded his arms over the back of the chair before he started talking.

"I'mma need you to keep this in mind—given the history between Phoenix and her dad and you and his old lady, whatever the slightest thing that goes wrong, it's going to be yo' fault."

Stokely was stunned. Cleve waved his hands and continued, "But you'll know it ain't yo' fault and they'll know it ain't yo' fault, but when folks get all confused with anger, fear, and whatnot, then blame becomes the knee-jerk reaction." Cleve reached for Stokely's shoulders and said, "Seems like these shoulders are strong enough to carry the blame."

Stokely was confused, but Cleve pressed forward. "Now see this how you gonna play it—don't push back. If it's a little something you can fix, go on ahead and handle the thing. If it's something totally unfounded, just kind of apologize and keep it moving."

Inklings of understanding began taking shape in Stokely's mind as Cleve continued, "See son, you walking into a storm that ain't really yours. It's theirs. But Phoenix can't be mad at you for Tanya, and she can't be mad at Tanya either. But all the uneasiness she feels about her past without her dad and however she responds to seeing him in the shape he's going to be in—all that? She's gonna need an outlet."

Cleve paused so that Stokely's comprehension could catch up. He went on, "The truth is she knows it's not your fault and that she recognizes you're by her side during one of her toughest times. So check this out, you... " Cleve pointed directly at his son. "In this storm, you are going to be like palm trees instead of rigid oaks; still standing when the storm is over." Cleve started swaying his body, "You're going to bend and sway with the storms. C'mon, do it with me, son."

Slowly, Stokely started to sway.

Cleve added, "She come at you in hysterics."

Stokely swayed to the side.

"She start bawling in tears of anger about her dad."

Stokely swayed some more.

"Tanya gets a little nostalgic."

Stokely swayed really hard.

Which prompted Elaine to burst into laughter from the doorway as both men sat in their chairs swaying from side to side.

Cleve responded, "What's funny? I gotta get him ready."

Stokely continued to sway from side to side, and Elaine laughed harder.

HE PULLED HIS TRUCK INTO THE DRIVEWAY AND EXHALED A deep sigh. Phoenix mumbled, "This is a nice house." To which Stokely responded in a measured tone, "Yeah, it looks cozy." Phoenix turned to him and he reached for her hand.

"Honey," he took a deep breath and added, "I'm with you."

She shook their hands and gave a half-smile. Stokely got out of the truck and headed around to let her out. Moments before they rang the doorbell, Tanya opened the door and hugged them in a group hug. With her keys and purse in hand and a hurried tone, she shared that not only would Oscar be happy to see them but that the health aides were here should they need anything. She was talking over her shoulder as she headed toward her car and said she should be back in a few hours.

Phoenix watched Tanya walk away and then turned to face Stokely, who had turned to look inside the house. "Is she always like this?"

Stokely faced her and replied nonchalantly, "Well, she is a determined spirit." Before Phoenix could ask anything else, Gregory, the health aide, welcomed them inside.

10

IF I COULD TURN BACK THE HANDS OF TIME

Tyrone Davis

May 1972

Cleveland punched the pastor.

What started with him accompanying Elaine to Bible Class at her biological father's church ended with some dislodged dentures as well as some spittle and blood on the pastor's shirt and Elaine feeling a triumvirate of uneasy emotions: fear, anger, and safety.

Cleve and Elaine were the only guests during the sparsely attended service. The underwhelming devotional service consisted of several "Test-a-lies," a phenomenon of exaggerated life experiences shared during the testimony part of the service. And when the head and only deacon called on the guests to introduce themselves, the handful of parishioners just could not make any sense of why these funny sounding Detroit Negroes would be in their church on a Tuesday evening. Not one of them could recall a time when they had a guest from somewhere farther than Memphis. The pastor was curious also, but he wouldn't let on.

Two hours later, Cleve wondered if the altar call was

perfunctory or did the pastor really believe his shallow inter-
pretation of Satan'stempting of Jesus had really stirred someone's soul. Cleve's surprise was palpable when Elaine stood
and made her way toward the front, a move that greased the
pastor's ego-driven pontification.

"My sista, GEES-us, done led ya from da DEE-troit dark-
ness to find da light right here in Ar-CAN-saw!" He
guffawed, and the deacon shouted, "Amen!" The pastor
continued, "No matta how deep in da muck and da mire yose
in, my Lawd will shine da light and lead ya' home!" Shouts of
praise came from the audience.

Elaine dryly asked, "But will you welcome me home …"
There was a little pause before she murmured the word that
would fuel the rural gossip mill from then on, "Daddy?"

The parishioners hushed so suddenly that if the shouts of
praise had been a vinyl record, the needle would have
scratched all the way across it.

February 10, 2015

Oscar was awake when Phoenix entered his room. At this
time of day, there was an abundance of sunlight and warmth
emanating from the windows. As far as he could tell, he was
feeling fine. He had eaten. His wife and the health aide had
tended to him, and although this was normally his nap time,
he was not tired.

When she closed the door behind herself, Oscar thought
he was dreaming. He rubbed his eyes and shook his head as
she approached slowly.

Through an impromptu parch of his vocal chords, a name
he hadn't uttered in some time escaped his throat, "Denise?"

Phoenix heard him and didn't have the emotional power
to correct him. She simply took a few strides to stand over
him at the side of his bed.

"I'm so glad you're here." Oscar's voice trailed off. He was confused. He gathered some bearings and asked, "How did you find me? Did you know I was sick?" He looked away for a moment before asking the scariest question, "Am I dying?"

There was a civil war raging in Phoenix's heart. On one hand, there was an immense blend of sadness and pity, and on the other hand, there was anger and resentment. The combat between her emotions constricted her voice and left her with just enough power to slowly extend her hand.

With a surge of relative power, Oscar clasped it quickly and tightly. He tugged, as if inviting her to sit. She sat near the edge with an abundance of tentativeness.

"Denise..." The pause in Oscar's words was accompanied by a slow tear trailing down his cheek. "You deserved better." A slight twitch in his hand caused him to do a sudden squeeze of Phoenix's hand. "I... I... " Regret rumbled through his heart like tennis shoes in a drying machine.

Phoenix's awareness was soothed when he resumed speaking, "I was so immature." Contemplation would best describe his expression as he added, "selfish, even." Then he fell into a little reflective pause before clarifying, "Very selfish to be exact." His upward glaze fell down on Phoenix and he peered closer. He took a deep breath before continuing, "Denise, you've always been so pretty and, and... and I'm here dying and you're there looking more youthful and more beautiful than I remember." He looked down at her hand as more tears welled in his eyes. He clutched her fingertips.

After wiping his nose with his other hand, a small smile emerged as he asked, "How's Phoenix? Our baby? How is she doing? Does she know I'm dying?"

Tears began to fight for release from Phoenix's eyes, but the pursing of her lips served as the last bastion of resistance to keep them at bay. She nodded a quick "yes," sniffled, and added a soft, "She's okay."

Oscar's countenance sank. He bit his lip and turned away. "She probably hates me" were the last audible words Phoenix could make out as Oscar began to sob. Her civil war of emotions would not allow her to hug him as she would normally do when consoling someone nor could the little girl inside of her release her father's hand.

The tears of regret continued, the sobbing slowed, and Oscar went on, "She would never understand." More tears ensued, "She probably thinks what I did is her fault." With a weak, but frantic sounding voice he turned to her, "Denise, it wasn't her fault. It was never her fault. Does she know that? Denise, does she know?"

Phoenix pursed her lips as tightly as possible and tightened her throat. She was not going to cry. She just offered the slow "Yes" head nods even after Oscar turned away.

In more than a whisper but weaker than an off-brand wet paper towel, Oscar asked rhetorically while looking away, "Do you think she'll come see me? Come see me before ..."

He was still looking away and would not see the slight sliver of liquid sadness trail along the side of Phoenix's face.

May 1972

As if seizing a deadly attacker, the pastor forcefully placed both hands on Elaine's head and shouted, "Fadda God, rebuke this demon of discord!" The deacon extended his hands upon Elaine's shoulders as the pastor continued his passionate prayer of casting out Satan's imps while the church members began to wail in prayer.

In a span of minutes, Cleve's emotional barometer moved from bored to wonder, to uncertainty, and when he saw these two dudes handling his wife, jerking her back and forth —his barometer moved into the red zone of anger and action.

In a handful of strides, he covered the distance from the pew to the altar. The wailing saints hushed as the pastor extolled, asking the Lord to form a hedge around this lost sinner. Cleve pushed the deacon, who was stunned and appalled. Then Cleve grabbed the pastor's wrist after seeing Elaine's face contorted with befuddlement. The pastor, who had taken on quite a crazed possessed expression himself, shouted, "All de devils in Hell can't stop my God!"

And that's when Cleve punched him—a right uppercut to the jaw. The parishioners parted like the Red Sea as Cleve led Elaine away from the altar and towards the door. One frightened member held out Elaine's purse and Cleve snatched it as they proceeded out of the sanctuary.

Before the doors closed behind them, Elaine turned free and took in the scene of a man who never acted on his parental responsibility to her, who draped his misdeeds with the language of the Bible, and who attempted to shame the truth when it was presented to him. There he was, holding his bloodied mouth, staring at her with a look of fanatical bewilderment and possibly misunderstanding that the blow he took was a reminder that sometimes the truth hurts.

An hour later, as Cleve steered his Camaro cautiously northwards on Highway 79, Elaine sliced through the silence with a declaration that was as final as it was certain: "Mister Cleveland Robeson, I can fight my own battles."

Cleve wanted to respond, rebut, and go on about some jive turkey handlin' his old lady. However, if he missed the drafty iciness of her tone, the ominous steadiness of her glare told him that this was not a matter of debate. He downshifted the gears, looked at the road ahead, then back at his wife, before nodding his head in acquiescence.

11

WHAT'S HAPPENING BROTHER

Marvin Gaye

February 11, 2015

Cleve and Elaine were seated together on Dr. Daniels' couch. Since their last visit, they agreed to proceed through counseling as a couple. Elaine knew that Cleve would benefit. She also knew he would never undertake this endeavor on his own. To him, helping her was more of a priority than helping himself. Which made Elaine feel secure and cared for, yet over the years, she became more and more convinced that his prioritizing others over himself may be his undoing.

Dr. Daniels angled, "When we last spoke, you talked about your father and you also mentioned a twin. Where is he?"

Cleve let out a long sigh, leaned back, and rubbed his hands on his thighs. He looked at Elaine and took a deep breath. "Remember STRESS?"

Dr. Daniels looked unsure.

"STRESS? Those cops back in the '70s, that was..." emotion clasped Cleve's vocal cords, but he regrouped. "Those cops that were targeting and killing young brothers."

Remembrance lighted upon Dr. Daniels.

Cleve pointed at nothing, but maybe in his mind he saw something. While pointing, he said, "Yeah, Columbus was one of their victims." He continued to make a yes motion with his head even after he had finished speaking.

Elaine was pained by the memory and troubled by the anguish she could see building within Cleve. A professionally empathetic Dr. Daniels asked for a little context. Cleve did a little laugh to keep from crying as he reached for Elaine's hand and asked, "'Laine, ever told you how me and her met?"

Dr. Daniels smiled and replied, "Yeah," she laughed, "Detroit was going up in flames and you two made a love connection." They all laughed nervously. Cleve's eyes drifted as he recollected those times. "So maybe you know, after things slowed a bit, 'Laine came back with me. Me and Columbus had us a cold water flat over on the North End. Really, it was a duplex with me upstairs and him below. Me and Bus worked over at Dodge Main, and he had kinda kept up a little side gig over at Mr. B's, a pool hall where we worked growing up."

The ladies let Cleve bask in the warmth of his memories as it appeared he was reliving the times. He continued with his disjointed story, "You see, Mama had died our last year at Northern, and Bus stopped going, but I managed to graduate. While I was still going to school, he spent nearly his whole day at Mr. B's."

Dr. Daniels made a note to revisit how casually Cleve mentioned his mother's death. Maybe he is focused on Columbus' story, or maybe it's something deeper. She continued listening.

"Even after I got him on at Main, he still made time at Mr. B's. I mean, ain't nobody ever said so, but folks nowadays would see him like the manager or something." It was obvious that the memories had transported Cleve beyond

Dr. Daniels' office. He clapped his hand and smiled, "One time, I guess, Bus had done really cleaned up with his hustle. Me and 'Laine and Bus and some gal—we was all at the Twenty Grand. We even heard some Motown cats, so you know we had a good time!" Cleve laughed. "It had to be right after Christmas '71, 'cause we was celebrating me and 'Laine getting married." Elaine rubbed his arm as she too had become enraptured by the memory.

Then, slowly, like watching a feather descend from the sky, Cleve's countenance fell. "The ladies went to the ladies room and Bus whispered how he had got in with these fellas and Mr. B's was like their pick-up spot, you know, for a cap of girl or a little reefer." Cleve looked to the floor. "Bus was saying this was an easy way to get some more stash in his slide and I just listened, you know." He sighed, "I mean, Bus could always flip a buck into two, you know what I mean?" He shook his head slowly. "See the thang is, I said we went to The Twenty Grand right to celebrate the wedding and 'exactly one year later, we buried Bus." Cleve inhaled a chest full of air and exhaled slowly, "Them ole punk-ass STRESS muthafukas they say Mr. B's was a 'place of ill-repute' and used that excuse to raid the place." Cleve shook his head in disbelief as he proceeded. "Would you believe there was no record of arrest from the so-called raid?" He looked at Elaine as he recalled the painful memory. "This is what we know: Bus was escorted out in handcuffs and a week later, his body was retrieved from a dumpster."

Cleve exhaled slowly. "All of the bullet wounds were front-entry, including those in his palms." Dr. Daniels listened in disbelief. "Yeah, exactly, how does someone get shot in their palms?" Elaine rubbed Cleve's hand and then his back. "Like, what they did to that boy at the playground..."

"Tamir Rice?" Dr. Daniels added.

"Yeah, Tamir Rice. Lil' man didn't stand a chance," Cleveland lamented. "I feel for his mother. She sends him out to play and he doesn't come back? Kids can't even play no more these damn police act like it's hunting season." He paused before adding. "You know what makes it worse? The whole regular day feeling to it all. Tamir's mom says, 'go play.' I tell 'Bus, 'Don't take no wooden nickels.' You know, a regular day that turns into a nightmare that you never saw coming." Cleveland's personal pain was also a collective pain, one in which both Elaine and Dr. Daniels could feel the palpable anguish of sudden tragic loss.

After a period of silence, Dr. Daniels asked, "How did you grieve?" Cleve's distorted expression conveyed his confusion. Daniels continued, "You have every reason to be angry about how your brother was murdered." At this point, she leaned forward and grasped Cleve's hands. Cleve deliberately avoided eye-contact. "But Cleveland, did you grieve your loss?"

He was looking away while pointing at Elaine. "'Laine said if we helped Coleman Young get elected, then he would do something about STRESS." Cleve let out a long exhale. "We went door to door with campaign stuff," a faint smile and chuckled escaped as he looked at Elaine. "We got a couple peoples to register and vote for the first time. Mayor Young won and busted up STRESS, but still... "

"That's not what I'm asking Cleveland. Helping Mayor Young was you doing something, something good in fact." She gently shook his hands as she made her next point, "But that is not grieving." He looked at Elaine and then at Dr. Daniels. "Your father, your mother, and your brother—you lost your whole family..." Dr. Daniels did a little fishing with her next comment to see how he would respond, "You lost them, tragically." His lips tightened, cueing Daniels to save the mother's death for a different time. She used the small opening to drive home her point, "Carrying that sadness, even if you hid it away, carrying it wears on your soul." She paused before adding, "And it would not surprise me if those pains were manifesting in your health." Cleve's shoulders slumped.

12

THANKS FOR MY CHILD

Cheryl Pepsii Riley

February 11, 2015

More often than not, vanity is a bad thing. It can be a source of disillusion and an obstruction to healthy relationships. It can cast a glossy sheen over shortcomings and impair objectivity. Vanity is a briar patch of pricks and needles that scars whomsoever becomes enmeshed and punctures the careless. However, every once in a while, amid vanity's thorns and thistles, a flower blooms. Among a mother's vanities, that flower is the awareness that her daughter is becoming the best of what she dreamed to be.

The flower blooms a little fuller when others recognize mom's brilliance within the daughter. Phoenix's flower sprouted beyond the briar patch of her mother's insecurities and vanity. Although she was recounting to her mother what happened during the visit with Oscar, the statement, "He thought I was you," pleasantly paused time, warmed a heart, and spurred a memory.

Fall 1980
Grambling State University

DENISE WAS NUDGED BY HER ROOMMATE, DELORES, YET KEPT her steady stride. The cafeteria was closing soon, and while an afternoon at the football game is fun, starving overnight was not. Denise walked forward with determination.

"Slow down, girl. I think someone wants to talk to you," Delores said, playfully. "Look, I don't have time for..." The rest of the statement never left Denise's mouth. Oscar Rosseau stepped in front of her. She, like numerous girls, debated whether Oscar was the new guy in the singing group, Shalamar. Those who said he wasn't thought so because Oscar was significantly more handsome. Plus, some people swore he was on campus the same day Shalamar was on *Soul Train*, so Oscar couldn't be that guy. But he was the guy in front of Denise, and the allure of his cologne made her forget about the cafeteria.

"Denise," he began, and Denise was overwhelmed with confused joy that he already knew her name. He went on, "I was watching you and wanted to know if you ladies could come over with us for a few minutes." Things were going well until he followed with, "Yeah, you can come sit on my lap and we can talk about the first thing that pops up."

And with that, his credibility took a tumble, and Denise remembered the cafeteria.

"You are going to have to do better than that," Denise responded, full of cockiness that could only be acquired from an upbringing in Vallejo, California.

"Damn mama, whatcha want me to say, 'will you marry me?'" Oscar retorted in an effort to regain some semblance of cool.

"Where my ring at then?" Denise replied with a sarcastic smirk.

Oscar's fraternity brothers began laughing so loudly that Oscar had to join in. With a reply that matched his cool persona, he added, "Just tell me where the chapel is and I'll be there in my tuxedo." Denise laughed a forgiving laugh.

"MAMA, WHAT'S SO FUNNY?" PHOENIX ASKED.

The question brought Denise back to the present. "Oh, nothing, honey. I'm headed home from the YMCA and this guy is out here on Kercheval dancing for money. I'm sorry, you were saying, Oscar thought you were me."

"Yeah, it was weird. Especially when he started talking about me, to me, thinking that he was talking to you." Denise could not conjure an appropriate response, so she inserted a soft "Ooohhh" to keep the conversation going.

In an effort to mask her sad confusion, Phoenix turned the conversation another way: "I think he still loves you. Even in his fragile state, there was a happiness that came over him when he thought he saw you." Phoenix smiled at the recollection before adding, "I don't know what happened between you and him, but you really made a big impression on him."

AS DENISE DROVE TOWARDS HOME, SHE SMILED AT TWO thoughts. The first was how Phoenix had mastered Denise's habit of smoothly changing the subject, and the other was the idea that Oscar still had feelings for her. Over the years, and with the help of a therapist, Denise came to learn and accept that Oscar's abandonment of their marriage was more about him and had little to nothing to do with all the self-imposed inadequacies that she heaped upon herself as a means to explain his departure. The mean internal dialogue she created about herself did more damage to her spirit than the abruptness of Oscar's leaving. Any woman who pays attention can recognize when something has changed, when a rift has formed, and when a split is imminent. Like many others, Denise resorted to blaming to help her make sense of things, and every day she impaled herself with the blame sword. But at that moment, listening to her daughter, she was reminded of what the therapist told her: "His choice is not an indictment of who you are."

MY LIFE

Mary J. Blige

February 11, 2015

Songhai was dizzy from overthinking.

Her mother always emphasized the approach of listing the pros and cons, which in this circumstance contributed to Song's dizziness.

She was correct about a website introducing their plumbing business to a wider audience. However, the call from the Interim Emergency Manager of Detroit Public Schools was not exactly the type of customer she had envisioned.

She tempered her thoughts of how much of a high-paying job this could be with the fact that they had not officially secured the contract. They could stand to make more money with this one job than what they usually made in month. But considering how DPS treated her mom, Song is pretty sure Cleve would pass on the job just on general principle.

However, optimism is one of Songhai's strongest traits. It sustained her during prison. It motivates her as she shapes a new identity after prison. And it compelled her to act on the

Interim Emergency Manager's idea that he could have someone open up the school so that they could walk around, see what was needed, and begin formulating an estimate. That was really a job for Cleve, a master plumber, but Song figured she would make a cursory visit to gather information with the hope of presenting her father with details that would inform his choice to take on the job.

McKenny Elementary School was not far from where Songhai grew up. Although it had been closed for a few years, the job would consist of making sure it was up to code for a possible sale. Driving through the neighborhood conjured some pleasant childhood memories. She could see herself and her buddies riding their bikes in the streets. She recalled hours of Double Dutch. She snickered at being the best basketball player for several blocks around, much to the chagrin of the boys. Those memories lightened the mood and cheerfully guided her steps to the door, where she was told to meet the DPS guy at noon. Even her pounding on the door carried a rhythmic giddiness that was infused with the possibility of securing a high-paying job.

The opening of the door and subsequently recognizing the maintenance man created a sinkhole in Songhai's heart that swallowed all her optimism and washed away every morsel of hope.

His block head was a dead giveaway, particularly where his forehead hooded his eyes in a nefarious darkened manner. His skin was duller than she remembered and the tattoo tears that he must have gotten in prison were just as faded as the sheen of his skin. When he spoke, the chipped front tooth was still there, hiding behind chapped lips. How on earth did she ever date such a specimen? Even back then, he had a menacing disposition that sent red flags flying everywhere.

Man-Man chuckled as he came face-to-face with his old girlfriend, the original ride-or-die chick. Her orangish red hair was an instant reminder. But unlike the sooty effect prison had on him, Songhai seemed more beautiful than he remembered. Granted, he had not laid eyes upon her since their sentencing, yet he could not grasp that he had ever dated a woman so beautiful. How did he fuck that up?

He followed his chuckle with, "So we meet again." In real time, the pause may have fallen between five and ten seconds, but in Songhai's mind and its movie reel of memories and consequences, the moment seemed much longer. When she replied, "Hello Ernest," it was devoid of any longing for lost love. In fact, during the eternity that elapsed, Song admitted that she never loved Man-Man and that dating him was the worst example of seeing the good in everyone. Even when there was little good to be found, Songhai's optimism uncovered some redemptive crumb of promise. However, at this moment, there was no doubt that standing before her was proof of her dumbest choice ever.

"Gurl, you know you ain't gotta call me Ernest. Just call me, Man; you know, like you used to." Man-Man had no inkling of all the regret bubbling in Songhai's spirit and in his typically block-headed way, he plowed forward. "Had they told me I was meeting you, I woulda got suited and booted." He laughed at his own joke.

Song found nothing amusing. All of the churning in her soul would not allow her to hate him, but she damn sure did not ever want to see him again, and certainly did not want to be alone with him. "Dontcha wanna come on in and get to work? It's cold out here, girl." Song was not conscious of the step she took backwards in response to the invitation. "Aw, don't tell me I drove all the way over here and my angel don't even wanna come in and do work." Then he licked his lips to relieve their dryness, but it came across as calculating in a creepy old man kind of way.

Amid the regret and discomfort, Song became resolute to not go inside. Ernest continued, "Ever since I got out, I changed. Got this job. Got me a little son. Shit, I even pay taxes." He laughed but Song was not amused. Not only was she not going inside, she accepted that this job and however much it would pay would not be worth the anguish. "Ain't you gonna be proud of me? I'mma changed man!"

Song took two steps back. "Why you like this, girl? I'm out here spillin' my heart to you and shit, you ackin' like you done seen a ghost!" About that, he was right. Song felt as though she was face-to-face with the worst mistake of her life and Ernest was a mutated version of Dicken's ghost-of-mistakes-past. The irony that he would be the doorman told Song what she had been ignoring all along; this job was one to pass on.

"Ernest, Man, it's good things are working out for you. I'm going to talk this over with my dad and call downtown if we need to reschedule. Right now, though, I've got to go."

Both of them knew she was talking about more than just the job. As she walked away, the futility of calling out to her muffled what Man-Man wanted to say. He knew they should have never been together, and he could never imagine how much she regretted that choice. But damn, she sure was fine.

CAN WE TALK

Tevin Campbell

February 13, 2015

L eaning on the lessons from his father, Stokely swayed with or, better yet, adjusted to Phoenix's silence. Her normal chattiness has been non-existent for most of this trip. Short answers and head nods made up the bulk of her communication. However, her body language told a different story. She was unusually clingy, especially when they were asleep. Quite regularly, while he drove, she would quietly reach for and hold his hand without looking at him—until now.

They were approaching Louisville when she asked, "What's one of your favorite memories with your father?" Stokely was slightly surprised at the sudden break in silence. He pondered for a moment, then launched into a story.

"When I was little, we used to live over by Seven Mile and Lasher." Phoenix chuckled.

"What's so funny?" Her glance contained that girlish merriment that he loved about her. "You really know someone is from Detroit when they say, 'Lash-sher' even though it's clearly spelled and pronounced 'Lahser.'" Stokely added, "Yeah, they meant Lasher so we just went on ahead and corrected them without charging them for it." Phoenix laughed for the first time in days.

"So yeah, it used to be a YMCA on the corner of Seven Mile and Lash-sher," Stokely added with comical emphasis. "And dad would take me and Song there to swim."

Phoenix, who had turned in her seat with her back resting on the door and her left leg tucked under her right knee, asked, "For swimming lessons?" Stokely, noting her attentiveness, replied, "Nawl, Dad had already taught us to swim. When we were there, it was like a fun time." Stokely paused as he recalled specific memories. "The one summer he was laid off, we went every day. But going back to what you asked, all of us would be at the pool and Dad would do his swim workout." Stokely was now immersed in memory. "Yo, when he did the butterfly—that shit was so poetic, I mean, you know like in a body symmetry kinda way. You could see all his muscles when he rose up out the pool. It was like, you know, how movies do like a slow-motion sequence of the hero in action?" Phoenix nodded. "That's how dad looked to me. When I think about being like my dad, that's the image that comes to mind."

Phoenix was warmed by how the memory impacted Stokely. Instead of regretting memories she didn't have, she saw his reaction as an indicator of the type of father he would be. She aimed to extend the warmth by asking, "Did you guys play baseball or football too?" Stokely laughed loudly before proceeding, "Well, we played basketball and Song whipped my ass every single time. Do you hear me?" He stretched out the syllables, "Ev-Ver-ree sin-gle time!" Phoenix laughed along, imaging little Stokely's discontent. "I mean, Song was all-state in her junior and senior years. She could beat all the dudes in the neighborhood." Phoenix eyes widened as she not only admired Stokely's support of his sister but also pictured Song as Monica from *Love & Basketball*.

Stokely was on a roll. "I remember the first time she beat dad. She was twelve and was crossing him over and raining jumpers on him!" They were both laughing. "Dad came into the house all exasperated, trying to explain shit, but me and Ma were watching from the window and witnessed that ass-whipping. He was trying to act like he had pulled his hamstring, but we knew the truth."

After the laughter subsided, Phoenix added, "Thanks for taking this trip with me." Stokely was slightly stunned and stumbled towards a reply, "Yeah baby, you're welcome. I'm glad you let me come." Phoenix reached for his hand and took a deep breath, "Can I tell you something?"

Stokely glanced at her and then back to the highway ahead. Aw shit, you got a viscous jump shot, too?" They laughed together. "I am pretty nice with it, but no." She shook his hand and looked away. "To avoid thinking about the relationship I didn't have with my dad, I worried about you and Tanya." Stokely could hear his father telling him to "Hush." He allowed Phoenix the space to process her thoughts. "I can definitely see why you were attracted to her and I think I understand how you were an escape for her." Stokely remained tight-lipped. "I believed you when you said it was over, but as a woman, it was reassuring to see confirmation from her side."

Stokely gripped the steering wheel tighter as he continued to stay silent. "I really can't imagine what it is like for her to be married to my father. I guess if he had the habits with her that he had with my mom, that would certainly make space for you." In his mind, Stokely started swaying back and forth like he had been coached. "Anyway, avoiding thinking about my dad stresses me more than I ever admitted." If she had been looking, she would have seen Stokely's expression as "Yeah, I see how you could say that," but she was focused on her own catharsis.

After a moment of silence, she resumed, "When daddy thoughts come up, I'll replace them with my kids in the swimming pool with their father." She smiled at Stokely, who asked, "You not going to be in the pool with them?" To which Phoenix responded, "Maybe sometimes, depends on how I'm wearing my hair." They both laughed. "Plus, kids deserve some special memories that are just between them and their dad, don't you think?" Stokely smiled and said, "I think I need to tighten up my butterfly stroke so our kids will have something to remember."

Phoenix heard, "Our kids," and it was the most encouraging thought she had all day.

YOUR DADDY LOVES YOU

Gil Scott-Heron

February 13, 2015

After wrapping up a water line repair, Cleve opted for lunch at home since they weren't too far away. Since Song has been working with her dad, she has come to enjoy their lunches together. For both of them, the conversations were akin to getting back lost time. It provides Cleve with "Daddy Time" and allows Song the comfort and safety of being a Daddy's girl.

When they arrived home, Cleve began sandwich preparation as Song turned on the TV. The broadcasters were wrapping up a speculative segment about Donald Trump exploring a run for president. Song announced, "Ain't nobody gonna vote for him. He's never even held an office." To which Cleve responded, "True, but don't let these White folk fool ya', they'd elect his ass just to get back at Obama." The idea caused father and daughter to look at each other in restrained horror.

Then the news anchor announced that they were going to switch to a live feed of a press conference held by the Interim

Emergency Manager of Detroit Public Schools, Mr. Wellington Shelby. Before the switch, the news anchor commented, "DPS is in a bit of turmoil. Hopefully this will be promising news."

Speaking from a podium at the district's main office, Mr. Shelby was flanked by Reverend Thigpen, who stood behind him on his right side. Mr. Shelby tapped the microphone and tugged at his French-cuffed sleeves before speaking.

"The executive team and I have been reviewing contracts and were appalled to find that, in addition to incomplete or shoddy work, the majority of the contracts were with companies outside the city." He pointed his finger emphatically when he said, "They have been underserving our kids and taking money from the city. But today we say ENOUGH!" When he said "we," he gestured between Reverend Thigpen and himself.

Cleve began laughing as he told Song, "Our friend thinks Reverend Charlatan has his back? Sheeeeeiiiiitttt, this won't end well." Cleve calling the man that name made Song wonder if this was the person who gave her mother hell. She was about to ask for confirmation when Cleve held up a finger as he watched the television.

Wellington Shelby held up a stack of papers and pronounced, "These are the contracts of those leeches and..." he ripped them in half. As he stared into the television cameras, Reverend Thigpen reached around Shelby's shoulder, picked up one half of the papers from the podium, and then tore that half into quarters. With a look of disgust, he dropped the torn papers to the floor and stepped on them as if extinguishing a cigarette.

"Our office has been contacting local minority-owned vendors to begin fulfilling these services," he said, shaking the other half of the ripped contracts in front of the cameras. "Not only will we reinvest taxpayers' money back into the city, we believe when our students see contractors that look like them, they will be inspired." He then puffed out his chest.

A reporter asked, "How does this improve student learning?"

Shelby responded with a look of surprise. "Have you seen some of our buildings? When those outsiders get away without doing work, they contribute to the physical deterioration of the places where our kids try to learn. We have to stop those thieves while providing quality facilities for our students."

Reverend Thigpen patted him on the back.

Another reporter asked, "Aren't those contracts legal documents? Won't the district have to address those matters in court?"

Shelby paused, and Thigpen reached over his shoulder and grabbed the mic. "You must be one of them. You must believe Detroit kids don't deserve a safe environment to learn. Where are you from, Lansing?"

The reporter sat down.

CLEVE TURNED DOWN THE VOLUME ON THE TV AND REPLIED, "That's some bullshit." He looked at Song, "That fool trying to curry favor with Black folk as he continues to shit all over the district. Next thang you know, he gonna be on our phone talkin' 'bout, 'are you a minority vendor?'"

Songhai swallowed hard, and Cleve paused. He tilted his head and squinted his eyes. He waited a second before slowly asking, "Did that fool already call you?" Like a child with a hand in the cookie jar, Song nodded a slow "yes." "I thought we were partners, Songhai. What's really going on?"

Songhai took a deep breath and said, "I spoke to him the other day while you and mom were at therapy. He invited us to take a look at McKenny and prepare a bid." Cleve was following along, nodding his head. "I figured you may not like the idea, so I went ahead to do a preliminary walk-through to see if I could come up with a reason for us to take the job." Cleve's eyebrows raised as if to say, "Oooohhhh."

Songhai exhaled a drawn out breath. "When I got there, the maintenance guy who was supposed to let me in," she sighed. "Well, I knew him." Cleve tilted his head the other way with a confused look. "It was Ernest." Cleve was still confused. "Man-Man, the boyfriend who I…" Song's shoulders slumped and her head lowered.

Cleve leaned back with his arms folded and pondered for a moment. Then he leaned forward and, with his fingertips, reached for Song's chin and raised her head. "Honey, you already done paid for that choice, you ain't gotta keep beating yourself up for it."

She wasn't crying, but the sad disappointment in her eyes could easily turn into waterworks. Cleve continued, "This is us, Song, me and you. What was ya trying to prove?"

Song responded weakly, "That I could bring big jobs to the table. I can do more for the business. That I …" Cleve cut her off, "Now I'mma tell you this—you, my partner, you ain't got to bring no big jobs to the table. I just need you to be you. Don't be devaluing what you mean to me, what you mean to the business. This business is doing better than it has done in years, and you know what's different about it?" He focused in on her eyes, "You. You are the difference maker. The business is better, I'm better, we're better because of you. Fuck that asshole and his bullshit minority contracts. Me and you, we got this."

Song was smiling as Cleve leaned back in his chair. Then he arched an eyebrow and pointed at her when he added, "So you saw old Man-Man's ass, hunh? I bet that confirmed your doubts." Song chuckled lightly, "It sure did."

16

TONIGHT, I CELEBRATE MY LOVE

Roberta Flack & Peabo Bryson

February 14, 2015

"No offense, Phoenix, but Stokes, y'all corny," Terrence said after they were seated at Flood's Bar & Grill. Everyone joined in the laughter, especially after Terrence got Steve in on the teasing.

"T, right man. You see, we been married long enough to not have to do the whole Valentine's Day song and dance." Steve reached across the table to give Terrence a fist pound. Then Terrence looked at Phoenix and Songhai and asked, "Speaking of which, why we gotta get y'all what y'all want but for our gifts we get what y'all want us to have?" Everybody laughed and Stokely added, "Yeah."

Wesley inserted, "Stokes, you might wanna sit this one out, dawg. Especially since Valentine's Day is y'all's anniversary." Songhai, who was seated beside Wes, added an "Amen" as she rested her hand on his shoulder.

Phoenix declared, "See, this is what women know." Everyone leaned toward her as she proceeded with a woman's truth, "We know what's best for us and what's best for you." Stokely, Terrence, Wes, and Steve threw up their hands in surrender. "Awwww hell nawl!" they shouted humorously as Songhai reached across the table and gave Phoenix a high five.

Terrence pushed it further, "What y'all high-fiving for? Song, where is your Valentine?" Song responded with a little embarrassment and a shoulder shrug. Terrence continued, "What you mean you don't know? You got a single dude right next to you and he done put on his best aftershave." Everybody cracked up. Wes flipped a middle finger at Terrence, who kept going. "See me and Steve, we know after a few drinks we gotta get back to our wives for a Valentine nightcap." Then he pointed at Stokely and Phoenix, "These two lovebirds, all chipper and shit." Then he turned to Wes and Song. "That leaves you two single folks up here acting all shy and shit. "Fuck the shy shit," he said as he elbowed Wes, "Shoot yo' shot man!"

All eyes turned to Wes and Song. Wes, who quite often quoted lines from movies, paraphrased *The Five Heartbeats* and responded, "Man, that ain't how you do Shy Brother." Then he turned to Songhai and asked, "Let's go dance and get away from these clowns." Song's blushing turned her cheeks the same reddish orange as her hair.

Terrence and Steve began gathering their coats as Terrence added, "Y'all ain't 'bout to have me up in this booth with y'all lovers like I'm Tag-Along Terry. I'm 'bout to bounce." He extended his fist for pounds as Steve said, "Y'all enjoy the first of y'all's anniversaries," which made Phoenix blush. Terrence and Steve resumed an earlier conversation as they headed to the door, "All I'm saying is I don't think Van Grundy is the best coach for the Pistons ..."

"They are a trip," Phoenix laughed as the gentlemen walked away. "Yeah, they are. I met them cats back in seventh grade and they ain't changed a bit," Stokely responded.

Phoenix leaned closer and asked, "What you think about 'the first of our anniversaries?'" Stokely kissed her and added, "I think I want to make that come true." Phoenix kissed him back.

To divert attention away from his arousal, Stokely asked, "You think Wes can give Song a ride home?" They both looked over to the dance floor and saw Wes and Song engrossed in their own groove. Phoenix responded, "Nah, I don't think he would object." They laughed as they watched what seemed to be childhood friends turning into a potential couple.

"Remember I told you Song could beat everybody in the neighborhood in hoops?" Phoenix nodded her head, which prompted Stokely to add, "Wes used to get served just like the rest of us." Phoenix looked at Stokely then back at the pair on the dance floor before adding, "Well, if I were a gambling woman, I'd bet Wes would be willing to get served tonight too." To which Stokely responded with playful jealousy, "My sister don't be serving people like that!"

Phoenix muffled a laugh by sipping her drink and looking back at the couple. Stokely's little brother jealousies were going head-to-head with his adult understanding of the value of healthy relationships. But Wes? Well, he knows Wes. So, does that make it better or worse? He didn't know, but when he looked over to Phoenix, he knew she was amused by his moment of conflicting emotions.

17

YOU HAVEN'T DONE NOTHIN'

Stevie Wonder

February 16, 2015

As the Interim Emergency Manager, Wellington
Shelby's primary responsibility was the fiscal
health of Detroit Public Schools—not the students,
teachers, or staff. His effectiveness in this role was determined by the governor and other statewide politicians, not
the parents, community members, or school board. Shelby
had a vague notion of the political quagmire in which he was
immersed. Guided by a faint understanding of the futility of
his position, he calmed his own fears by focusing on himself,
or as he would prefer to say it—his brand.

In an effort to reinforce or perhaps expand his brand, he
created a pseudo community meeting called "Mondays with
the Manager." He proclaimed that this would give parents
and others a chance to interact with him. During the executive administrators meeting, he even allowed the description
of "letting them touch the hem of my garment" to slip from
his lips. He attempted to frame the comment as a joke.
However, not one of the administrators could detect a kernel

of humor amid the abundance of presumptuous self-importance.

Shelby kicked off the first of these *Mondays with the Manager* meetings at Shuttlesworth Elementary School. The irony that a school named in honor of a hero such as Fred Shuttlesworth was led by a spineless moderate like Principal Wilkins roused the ire of local activists. It was Principal Wilkins' invitation that spurred Shelby's delusion of grandeur. It was also Principal Wilkins who approved the agenda for a community meeting with only one direction of communication, from Shelby to the audience. There would be no question and answer segment. When parents reviewed the agenda upon arriving, their cynicism grew.

Wellington led with a few formalities before launching into his rehearsed-to-appear-informal speech. "A lot of people have something to say about Detroit Public Schools. The newspapers' focus is on sensationally overblown matters to sell papers. Statewide politicians focus on test scores to validate their goal of overseeing our affairs. And the governor talks with great hope about our potential." Shelby paused for a moment to tug at his French cuffs and further straighten his back.

"But no one is better equipped to tell our story better than us." He looked around to see if anyone was listening. It appeared he had their attention, so he reached in his jacket pocket, retrieved his iPhone, and extended it toward the audience. The gesture caused one parent to reach beneath his sweatshirt and palm the handle of the revolver tucked into his waistband. Other parents leaned back in apprehension and disbelief because one simply does not suddenly reach inside jacket pockets and retrieve anything without garnering defensiveness from Detroiters.

Clueless of the ripple he caused, Shelby clicked his phone and opened the Twitter app. "Starting today, right now, we take control of our narrative. We will tell the stories of what's really going on. We will use social media to tell the world about the good things going on in DPS! Because in my opinion, if it's not on social media, it didn't really happen." With that he turned his back to the audience, extended his phone upward, and deftly took a selfie with himself looking serious in the forefront and the parents looking befuddled and skeptical in the background. Then he ignored the parents and tweeted the picture with the following caption:

We're serious about taking back our schools. #DPScomeback

The realization that nothing would be accomplished began to dawn upon the participants. Shelby resumed, "Be sure to use the hashtag #DPScomeback when you tell our story on social media. That's pound sign-capital D-capital P-capital S-lowercase -c-o-m-e-b-a-c-k. Do you people under-stand that? I will say it again, pound sign-capital D..."

A parent stood in exasperation, "Man, we don't care about no damn social media, we care about our kids!" To which Shelby replied, "Me too. That's why we need to tell our story!" Toward the rear, a quick-thinking parent whose patience was exhausted snapped a picture that featured the back of the standing parent pointing at Shelby, who was looking down at his phone. The parent who took the picture tweeted it with this caption:

We talk, they don't listen. We want an education for our kids, They talk down to us. That's our story #DPScomeback (?)

As disgruntled attendees began leaving the auditorium before Shelby could finish, the parent's tweet was retweeted multiple times. Two hours later, in his Midtown office,

Shelby tweeted a picture of him and Principal Wilkins shaking hands with a caption that read:

Loyal servants for the students of Detroit. #DPScomeback

After posting the tweet, he clicked on the hashtag to see if it had gained any traction. It had, but not the type for which he had hoped. The parent's tweet with the picture of Shelby preoccupied with his phone had been retweeted over five hundred times. Other tweets and retweets had taken a tone that further dampened Shelby's idealism. A few tweets with the hashtag read:

Wade Donald @MrDonald:
We were told things would change—but they haven't. #DPScomeback

Ms. Jackson @Jackyifyounasty:
Worst test scores in the state #DPScomeback

Angry Man @sitchoas_down:
48 kids in my daughters 3rd grade class—but who is counting? #DPScomeback

Karen Kennedy @suburbanmom
They should blow it up and start all over #DPScomeback

Boss Playa @stackthispaper$:
I'm tired of these ninjas talking about a comeback when they stealing the money #DPScomeback

Councilwoman Evers @councilwomanevers:
If interim manger Shelby doesn't come correct, he is going to see the real me from the Eastside. #DPScomeback

Dedicated Teacher @the1619projectisvaluable
Improved student achievement should be the focus and would be the best narrative of all. #DPScomeback

Hal O'Malley @randomangrywhitedude
I would not let my kid take a drink of water in that pigsty #DPScomeback

After reading those tweets and seeing the steady retweeting of the parent's unflattering picture of him, Shelby placed his phone down on his desk, exhaled a long breath, and slumped back in his chair. Oddly, he possessed the foresight to recognize that his failure would further entrench the state's colonization of DPS. He also naively believed that he was the only one who could stop it. He felt the need for guidance, a voice of reason and understanding. That need prompted a phone call to Reverend Thigpen.

18

SAID I WASN'T GONNA TELL NOBODY

Sam & Dave

February 17, 2015
Detroit

Dr. Daniels began the therapy session with an observation from her weekend.

"There is a point I want to share with the hope that it could provide a framework for today's conversation." Cleve and Elaine nodded in agreement, providing the cue for Dr. Daniels to continue.

"This past weekend, my son and I were talking, and he shared his frustration over his bank account." A statement that conjured parental chuckles from the trio and even spurred Cleve to jokingly inquire, "How much did he need to borrow?" They all laughed some more before Dr. Daniels continued, "Nothing this time—thank God—but he had a peculiar set of circumstances that were causing his discomfort." Cleve and Elaine exchanged looks of interest. "It seems that he has a number of subscriptions to streaming, cloud, and other services that automatically deduct from his account each month. Many of the subscriptions he had forgotten he had. " Elaine nodded in a manner that would serve as a church member's "Amen!"

Dr. Daniels went on, "I would like us to focus on the bank account of our souls." She paused so that the concept could sink in. "As humans, there is a tendency to subscribe to perceptions, beliefs, and limited views that consistently deduct from our soul account. What I want to do today is explore some of those deductions." Cleve and Elaine exchanged glances. "Cleve, you may recall me pushing you to acknowledge how or whether you grieved. You may also recall that you didn't have an answer. I'm suggesting today that what you did not grieve may be making deductions on your soul account." The couple nodded with growing understanding.

"I want to emphasize that acknowledgment is not judgement. We are not here to label how you feel. We are here to begin an assessment process that I believe can lead to healing and slow the deductions from your soul account." Dr. Daniels eyed both her patients and added, "Elaine, let's start with you. Can you name or identify possible deductions from your soul account? Something from which you can begin to heal?"

Nashville

Considering his unusual display of energy, Tanya pondered if this was the best time to inquire about things that Oscar had kept from her. When she approached him, he was seated and gazing through the bay window in their bedroom.

She draped an arm over his shoulder and kissed the top of his head as she headed to the opposite chair. With a parting caress, he briefly held her hand as she moved away.

When she sat, she looked at him so intently that he began to get uncomfortable.

"Oscar, why did you choose to avoid telling me about your daughter?"

Now he was very uncomfortable. He fidgeted in his chair and resumed looking out the window. He also added an additional lock to his spiritual closet of secrets. Tanya waited for what seemed an eternity before recognizing that he was stonewalling her with silence. She tried another angle.

"Weren't you surprised to see her last week?"

The question caused a bit of confusion. With a tone of defensiveness, Oscar stoically replied, "I did not see her last week." Tanya was shocked and raised her voice. "You did too! She came and talked to you in this room."

Oscar turned in confusion and said, "What are you talking about? In fact, I was meaning to ask you about that. How did you get in touch with Denise? Why did she come?" Now, Tanya was confused. She replied slowly, "Oscar, I don't know Denise. I did not get in touch with her. I got in touch with Phoenix and she came to visit you."

She allowed the memories to rewind in Oscar's mind. He did not say anything, but his expressions moved from bothered to disoriented to angry to disappointed. For clarity, he pointed to the floor and asked, "Phoenix was here?" Tanya shook her head, "yes," with an expression of serious concern. Oscar continued to contemplate.

"No, that is not right. I asked Denise about Phoenix and she said she was 'alright,'" Oscar replied with diminishing conviction. "No, Phoenix was not here. She would have had a bunch of questions for me." He was trying to convince himself. "She would only come to see me if I was dying or something." He looked to Tanya for confirmation. Tanya didn't flinch. He took another leap toward confirmation,

"How would you get in touch with Phoenix anyhow?" Clarity struck him like a lightening bolt.

"You reached out to your little boyfriend?"

Tanya laid her head back in exasperation. Not only was he going to avoid talking about Phoenix; he was going to attempt to guilt trip her in the process of dodging the question.

Detroit

"The situation with Andrette is deducting from my soul," Elaine replied with a whisper. "Apparently, she agreed to confront Reverend Thigpen during the sickout day my staff took in protest of how I was treated. Since then, no one has heard from her. The first few times I called, I left a message. Later, that phone line was no longer in service." Elaine looked down at the floor in disappointment.

Dr. Daniels inquired, "Andrette is one of the staff members who spoke up for you during the hearings, right?"

Elaine nodded.

"Are you saying that she is missing?"

"I do not want to say that. Nor do I want to say what I'm afraid may have happened to her."

Dr. Daniels looked at Cleve, who attempted an explanation, "Well Doc, you see, well um. Look, Andrette, she is, you know... " Cleve made confusing gestures with his hands before nearly whispering, "She is transgender." Cleve let understanding creep over Dr. Daniels. "And well, you know like, well, a lot of the trans folks, especially the lady ones, have been coming up missing and ain't nobody talkin' 'bout it."

Elaine jumped right in, "I went by the apartment where she stayed but she had been evicted. The landlord said she was behind on her rent but never moved out. He said he just let himself in and put her belongings on the curb where people started taking what they liked." The hopelessness Elaine felt began to pervade the room. "I was afraid that if I talked about it, maybe I was jinxing the possibility that she would show up."

Cleve added, "'Laine said one of the teachers filed a missing persons report but left the police station feeling more doubtful than assured."

"Andrette is a survivor. She survived Hurricane Katrina. She survived losing her family. And it seems she survived the trauma of being teased and picked on growing up. As far as I know, she didn't have family or close friends. But she was a part of our family and now it feels like we can't do anything about what has happened to her. Everybody is going on with their lives as if her life didn't matter." Elaine was raising her voice, "But Andrette did matter. She mattered to our kids. She mattered to our school. She mattered to me." Elaine sniffled. "Now, she is... oh, Lord knows where, and I." Elaine pointed to herself, "I feel so hopeless about getting her back."

The tears began to trickle down Elaine's cheeks.

Nashville

"Oscar, that is not the point," Tanya said with a simmering rage. "The daughter you concealed from me was here to see about your well-being, and you are acting as if she was her mother?" Tanya sighed, "I don't know whether to be confused or upset." She rested her head in her palms.

Oscar was avoiding the question in a peculiarly perverted way, fearful of the avalanche of unwanted emotions and memories that might ensue. The big boulder in that pending avalanche was his deep internal dialogue about having failed as a father. The negative dialogue was so pervasive and repetitive that, oddly, his choice to not talk about it made the metaphorical boulder bigger and the potential emotional avalanche more deadly.

Additionally, despite Tanya's career achievements, Oscar held onto some outdated patriarchal notions of his wealth and age, granting him some higher status in their relationship. It was not true, but Oscar liked to believe that Tanya was dependent upon him. This distortion added to the ignorance of his choice to not confide in his wife. Despite his high regard for her, he still did not grasp her full splendor. This is exactly the same mistake he made in his marriage to Denise.

HOPELESS

Dionne Farris

February 17, 2015
Detroit

C leve extended the box of Kleenex to Elaine, who grabbed a fistful. After seeing she had enough, he began, "'Laine ain't the only one wrestling with hopelessness." Cleve sat erect and rubbed his hands up and down his thighs. None of the reluctance to talk that he demonstrated during the first session was apparent. He was not only ready to share, he was ready to heal.

"My Papa was assassinated. My brother was murdered by the police. My Ma'Dear had life drained from her. My daughter was unfairly sentenced at best and railroaded at worst." Each time he spoke of a family member, he raised one hand and then the other. "Hopelessness has been with me throughout my journey."

Then he reached over and rubbed Elaine's thigh and added, "So has hope."

A blush emerged through Elaine's sorrow as she placed her hand atop his. "I don't think I grieved much and I'm hoping you can give me a few pointers on how; I have just sort of packed up and moved on. Like Mama did when we left Daddy's corpse dangling in the sun." Cleve exhaled a mangled sigh that reflected his effort to control his emotions. "You know how pretty the sun is first thing in the morning?" He paused so that the ladies could show agreement. "For me, that beautiful picture of a new day has an ugly stain down the middle. A big smear that matches the silhouette of my Papa hanging from that tree." He paused to take a deep breath. "And life is like Ma'Dear tugging on my arm as I look back, pulling me to go forward, to live on." Dr. Daniels found herself fighting back tears.

"Even though I didn't grieve ... yet," he held up a finger with a slight smile. "I have kinda made it this far by focusing. I focus on what I can do in this moment and then assure myself that whatever it takes to make it through the next moment, I'm prepared for it." He then pointed at his wife. "It ain't her job to make me happy. But when she is true to herself, I'm inspired. And I'm happy because she chooses to spend this time," he paused before adding, "And all these times with me." He caressed her hand and lifted it to kiss it. "What we have, what we've built, and the good feelings about what we can do—that is my dependable hope."

Elaine reached over to hug him.

Nashville

After Tanya left the room, Oscar's mind began replaying things he had never shared. Although the memories, fears, and pain often surfaced in his thoughts, he never allowed his tongue to grant them release. The confusion about whether Phoenix or Denise came to see him conjured the notion he associated with Phoenix: she would only visit him if he was dying.

He hung his head with the weight of decades of disappointment.

Disappointment that he learned from his mother to compartmentalize and suppress. He recalled how, as a child, he could hear his parents argue and how those arguments evolved into physical confrontations. Certainly, a child cannot comprehend the scope of parental discord, but Oscar developed the view that his mother was trying to do too much. She was getting out of her place. She was trying to take over and make his father a henpecked chump.

Although he disagreed with physical abuse and his attempts at commiseration with his mother came from a patronizing expectation that she should shut up and be happy with what she had, Oscar viewed himself as better than his father. He never hit Tanya or Denise. In this moment of reflection, he glossed over the fact that Tanya would prove a formidable foe in fighting back, and Denise, despite her size, would probably retaliate with the ferocity of a wolverine. Oscar avoided those truths and projected onto his wives his flawed expectation of his mother: stay in your place.

Detroit

"Cleveland, that's beautiful," Dr. Daniels responded. "Yet, we missed what may be deducting from your spirit." She was pushing Cleve beyond his comfort zone. "Allow me to share a different perspective with you because perhaps deductions is not the best frame for you." She paused to receive Cleve's nonverbal consent to continue. "Have you ever carried multiple inflated balloons in an extra large bag?" Both Cleve and Elaine conjured the image. "Now technically, there is still space in the bag, but realistically, the bag is full. Cleveland, let's consider your spirit as that bag. You've got a big heart and thus deserve a big bag." The couple chuckled. "What I think is a way to free up some space in your spirit and in your bag is to deflate the balloons." Understanding was dawning on the couple. "The balloons are the incidents over which you haven't grieved. You've coped. You've managed to live forward despite the drag of past trauma—something I am commending you for, yet I really want to impress upon you that it is possible for you to continue healing. It is possible to live more fully with less drag, with less of your energy being consumed and fewer deductions from your soul account. I believe that there is a release of air, of tension, of trauma when you discuss, acknowledge, or meditate upon each trauma-filled balloon. When you release the air from the balloons, they will still be in the bag—just as your memories will stay with you, but their accompanying trauma will take up less space in your spirit."

Dr. Daniels paused to let the concept sink in before adding, "Cleveland, as you implied, the love and life you and Elaine created with and for each other is a safe space, a haven for healing. What I hope for you going forward is some intentional healing. Releasing the air from the trauma balloons and canceling subscriptions that deduct from your spirit."

She added one more point. "Does Elaine know your mother's story?" Cleve was mildly unsure. "That's an example. I don't think you tried to deceive her. But I imagine, as a man who often has the answers, it is quite different to speak upon something to which you have no answers." Cleve looked at Elaine, who patted his hand. "Next time we meet, I'll ask Elaine what she knows about your mother." Dr. Daniels winked and smiled, "I suggest you take care of that homework."

Nashville

OSCAR'S RESOLVE WAS NOT THE ONLY THING HARDENING AS memories and negative dialogue replayed in his mind; so was the plaque in his arteries. Much like the building of debris along a narrow point in a stream, the life flow of water slows to a trickle until that final piece of debris wedges into place and damns life.

As the child of a well-to-do mortician, Oscar came of age with privilege and opportunity, but no paternal love. His father, after whom he was named, subscribed to the notion that fatherhood was solely providing. His wife, son, mistress, and their love child all had a house, food, and material trappings to show how well-kept they were. Little Oscar grew up with a lot of things, but was bereft of his father's attention, guidance, and love. He also grew up with blame by projecting onto his mother his anger over the shortcomings of his father.

Blessed with eye-catching handsomeness, Oscar would garner attention from many women. None of whom would garner access to his heart. It wasn't that they were untrustworthy or that they didn't put forth the effort; it was because Oscar had dug an emotional moat around his spirit to maintain distance and thus prevent another occurrence of the disappointment he experienced with his father. Even as marrying Denise and fathering their child seemed to almost bridge Denise's heart to his, fear and unresolved trauma spurred him to widen the moat, undermine marriage, and forsake fatherhood.

He recalled how, even as a toddler, Phoenix was a duplicate of Denise's determination as well as her beauty. He recalled having her in his lap while driving his new Corvette and her attempts at steering as if she knew how to drive. He also recalled allowing his military commitment to paper over his fear of marriage and parenting and become a convenient, albeit weak, excuse for why he could not be a husband or a father.

Oscar sadly recalled how his embrace of the military led him to the experience of what was then a novel concept— friendly fire. Soldiers in his charge may or may not have met their fate due to Oscar's choices. There was no formal investigation, but Oscar still indicted himself and burdened himself with blame and guilt.

His marriage to Tanya was to be an example of his new approach to life, and he did manage to remain married much longer the second time around. However, time, love, and Tanya's intentions could not traverse the moat, isolating Oscar's heart.

As surely as the last piece of debris damns a stream, the last plaguing particle solidified the blocking of his weakened arteries, and Oscar sat upright with a sudden epiphany —"Why? What was the value of being emotionally distant with his wives? Why was he unnecessarily guarded in sharing his health challenges? Why couldn't he accept that Denise, Phoenix, and Tanya were more than the little boxes in which he tried to contain them? Was he afraid? For Christ's sake, you're a soldier! You can survive bombings, hails of bullets, and other forms of battle, but you aren't man enough to trust someone who has pledged and demonstrated their commitment to you? Why Oscar? Why?"

As his body began to slump, the voice of internal dialogue shifted from his own to that of his mother's. In a flash, he was transported back to his childhood when he accidentally smashed his fingers after rummaging through his father's trunk. Not only had he broken a finger, but he bit his tongue so hard to keep from crying that it began to bleed. When his mother saw his purpling hand and the blood in his mouth, she embraced him tightly and then held him away at arm's length to survey the damage. Oscar refused to cry, but his mother could see the evidence of his self-inflicted wounds.

As Oscar saw it this time, his mother, youthful in appearance, was standing between his chair and the bay window. When Oscar rose to meet her "why" inquiry within the expanse of her open arms, he looked back to notice his closed eyes, bowed head, and slumped body remaining in the chair. When he turned again to his mother, she glowed more brilliantly, and the worried-edge of her asking "why" was replaced with the warmth of understanding. With one last look back, he saw his lifeless body and Tanya entering the room. He waved an unseen goodbye before stepping into the fullness of his mother's embrace. He was already gone before the scream escaped Tanya's throat.

ONE LOVE
Whodini

February 17, 2015
Detroit

Phoenix would be Ecstasy, with her headwrap serving in place of the rapper's leather Zorro hat, and Stokely would be Jalil.

They settled into this routine, with Phoenix perched on the bathroom countertop in her pajamas and Stokely standing bare-chested in front of the mirror as he shaved. Phoenix was DJing by selecting songs from Stokely's phone. The music was coming through the Bluetooth connection with the small speaker in her shower.

That Stokely's phone was synced to Phoenix's speaker was just another indicator of their relationship bond. There were sport jackets, workout apparel, and a variety of t-shirts of Stokely's in Phoenix's drawers and closets. In Stokely's apartment, along one wall, were his large size twelve boots, joined by a pair of Phoenix's size six and a half running shoes and house slippers. Evidence of their presence in each other's lives was apparent amongst their things, within their living spaces, and in their rapport.

"C'mon Phoenix, you just rapped all the bars from *Five Minutes of Funk*," Stokely laughed. "You do know that Whodini is a duo," he reminded her as he held up two fingers. Phoenix chuckled mischievously, "I know, I know. I'll do better this time." She cued Whodini's *One Love* and began her overly demonstrative reenactment as Ecstasy explained that love and like both contain four letters.

Much like the song's bridge in the music video when the group does the peculiar side-to-side choreography, Stokely stepped from side-to-side and Phoenix leaned heavily to each side while remaining on the countertop. She had winked at Stokely when he rapped Jalil's verse about being lucky to find one love. However, when he got to the line about losing his love because of cheating, the song was inter- rupted by an incoming call. Phoenix noted that the number was not saved and quickly pressed the decline button. By the time the song resumed and Stokely reached Jalil's bars about thanking the woman for teaching him love, the phone rang again from the same number. Phoenix made a pouty face and extended the phone to Stokely, who pressed the accept button and answered, "Hey, this is Stokely."

"Stokely?" the caller asked.

Stokely knew the voice, although he asked in response, "Tanya?" Phoenix made a perturbed face.

"Is Phoenix with you?"

All Stokely could say was, "Yeah, she's right…" Phoenix took the phone from his hand and wiped the shaving cream off the edges.

"Phoenix?"

There was a long pause.

"Your father…"

Phoenix's expression plummeted from bothered to saddened. She responded weakly, "No."

Tanya replied with a morose certainty, "Yes, earlier today." Before she could continue, Phoenix handed the phone back to Stokely, slumped off the countertop, and retreated to her bedroom.

Stokely fumbled the phone before placing it alongside his face, "Tanya? Oscar, he... he, did he... well, how is he?"

With a defeated sigh and a tone just louder than a whisper, "He... isn't doing. I'll be back in touch with the arrangements. "

"Ohhhh Tanya, I'm sorry." Stokely didn't want to go into an obligatory "If you need anything," cliche' so he repeated that he was sorry.

"Thank you," she answered, before adding, "I need to make a few other calls. Good night."

"Good night," he was sure she had already hung up before he said, "Night." But that didn't make any difference. He exhaled a long sigh, dipped his wash cloth into the warm water, wrung it out, and wiped the remaining shaving cream from his face. Then he looked in the mirror, shook his head slowly, sighed again, and made his way to the bedroom.

He found Phoenix sitting with her knees to her chest and her forehead resting on her knees, near the farthest edge of the bed, cornering the headboard. He walked around to that side, sat softly near her for a moment, before reaching out slowly to caress her bare foot. He did a little thumbing movement on her sole before she released her knees, leaned over, and wrapped her arms around his neck. Stokely noticed there were no tears or sniffles, just a heavy sadness. As he wrapped an arm around her, she repositioned herself to sit in his lap. He followed along and cradled her like a big baby. He even began an unsteady rocking as she nestled closer, aligning the bridge of her nose along his neck. She wiped away a small remnant of shaving cream and snuggled again. This time, tightening her arms around his neck.

The music resumed at this point, and Stokely heard Ecstasy advise how we should learn who is for real or fake, and that once we earn love, we must know how to keep it.

Stokely held her tighter, kissed her on the temple, and gained a more soothing rhythm by rocking her in his arms.

21

IF YOU DON'T KNOW ME BY NOW

Harold Melvin & the Blue Notes

February 18, 2015

Wednesday mornings meant mother-daughter time at the downtown YMCA. Denise was a little worried that Phoenix was later than usual, but she began her walk around the track with the certainty that her daughter would arrive soon.

By the time she rounded the second curve, she saw Phoenix, slump-shouldered, emerging from the locker room. As she neared, Denise opened her arms for an embrace. When she wrapped Phoenix in her arms, she asked, "Baby, what's going on?"

Phoenix whimpered, "Oscar."

Assuming the matter involved the unusual but expired love triangle between Phoenix's father, her boyfriend, and her father's second wife, Denise rubbed her daughter's back and consoled, "Oh baby, things will clear up as time passes."

Phoenix stepped back and dryly stated, "Mom, Oscar died."

For a moment, Denise was frozen as she and Oscar's

courtship and marriage replayed in her mind. Phoenix watched as her mother's expressions moved from smiles to sadness. When Denise's memories reached the point of young parenthood, she reached for Phoenix's hand to begin their walk. After a lap, Denise, who had begun to let go of slow and silent tears, asked, "Do you remember when I used to get so mad at you for not saying how you felt?"

Phoenix did not really remember. She remembered a handful of times when Denise was angry, but time had allowed Phoenix to forget the circumstances. Denise clarified, "Looking back, the particular incidents are of no consequence." She took a deep breath before continuing. "My real issue was the fear that you were repeating Oscar's worst habit."

Phoenix was confused, and her expression conveyed it obviously. Denise pumped their hands a few times without letting go and smiled beneath her tears. She nodded "yes" as she continued, "Your father would have never ever been described as self-revealing." Denise chuckled weakly, "Damn, I'm already using past tense." She wiped her tears with her free hand. "I never knew what was on his mind, what he was thinking. But I could kind of see, though, him erecting a higher wall that—silly me—I kept trying to scale."

Oddly, Denise channeled an old argument and pointed to herself, "But I'm your wife, Oscar, your helpmate!" She and Phoenix walked several steps before memories allowed Denise to return to the moment, "But he never shared. He never opened up. I am not even talking about reactions of anger; he was just closed off to me, period."

They walked another half lap before Denise continued, "Years after we divorced, I realized two things: his lack of communication wasn't about me and that all that bottled up emotion was going to choke the life out of him." Then she asked, "Do you know how he died?" Phoenix shook her head, "No."

Denise made a declaration out of the blue, "I think we—me, you, and Stokely—should attend the services." Phoenix's expression was confused and incredulous, which prompted Denise to stop walking and face her daughter. "Yep, that right there. That's a little of Oscar in you. There is no reason for Stokely not to go." However, Denise pressed ahead, "Oscar would push people away when he was in need and you, however you choose to grieve, should not adopt that practice." Denise pointed to herself and Phoenix, saying, "I've been grieving for years and I will need your support." Then she softly poked Phoenix, "Your grief will be a lot different and that's okay, but mother-to-daughter and woman-to-woman, allow your man to support you. Don't push him away when you're in need. That achieves nothing but mixed messages of misunderstanding." Denise tugged at Phoenix's hand to resume walking.

WES BEEPED THE HORN TWICE AS HE AND SONG PULLED AWAY from Odell's house. Song and Cleve had spent the day doing an assortment of small plumbing jobs around Odell's house as he stood over their shoulders talking non-stop.

When he and Cleve waved at the departing car, Odell added in his annoying nasal-pitched voice, "Thank God she took after her mother more than you," he chuckled. "Had she taken after you, she prolly neva get no date!"

They laughed as Cleve responded with a playful, "Fuck you, Dell!"

Anyone who saw the pair would have assumed that Odell was older than Cleve. His back had a noticeable drooping curve. Depending on the situation, he alternated between a cane and a walker. Odell was one of those alleged good-haired black men who, back in the 70s, got over with their not-quite-Billy-Dee-Williams look. Nowadays, the top of his head was shiny and bald, and the few strands of silver above his ears and down the back of his neck had been pulled into an un-moisturized ponytail.

"So you and old girl still kickin' it, huh?" Odell asked sarcastically. "What the hell you mean, Dell?" Cleve quipped with playful hostility. "Fool, you know that's my queen." Odell looked at his work buddy in disbelief while shaking his head. "Yeah, she whopped that thang on you so good you can't turn it loose." They laughed cautiously while Cleve became suspicious of what Odell wasn't saying.

"I 'member back when we was at Main and you gave up on the bitches for this here girl, talkin' 'bout you 'like her fire.'" Odell snorted, "Humph. We knows you was whipped just fa' sayin' some shit like that."

"Dell? I been married damn near fifty years. This bullshit you selling? I ain't buying," Cleve said firmly. "See that's what I'm sayin'! The same pussy for fifty years? Fuck that, I like to switch my hoes up. Gots ta' have three or fo' at any given time 'case one them bitches get courageous and I hafta stomp a mudhole in dey ass," Odell said with irrational bravado.

Cleve looked at his broken friend. Then he turned and looked at the dilapidated house and considered the work he and Song did, for which he undercharged Odell, who still complained. Cleve reflected on the parade of roaches that prompted Songhai to flee to the van. He recalled having to wear a mask to help adapt to the pervasive stench of urine throughout the house. Then he arched an eyebrow and asked, in disbelief, "What hoes you got, man? Ain't no woman been in that house for damn sure."

"Aw nawl Cleveland, pimps don't let hoes know where he lay his head. These bitches is scandalous. They'll get ya fa' all ya' got if ya sleepin'," Odell pronounced as if he had said something enlightening. "Dell, you ain't got shit," Cleve responded with more anger than he wanted to reveal.

Odell shouted, "Fool, I can still throw these thangs," as he released his cane and held up his fists. The cane fell to the ground, and the unsteadiness caused Odell to totter. Cleve retrieved the cane and handed it back to Odell, who replied, "Thanks. Now, like I was sayin' I don't be trusting these bitches. Be'fo ya know it, they'd have yo' ass watchin' Oprah and being all in touch wit ya' feelings and shit. Talkin' 'bout 'tell me how ya' feel honey. You can trust me.'" Then he spat in disgust, "All that ghey-assed shit is fuckin' up the game."

"Dell, dude, look at us. We too old for the game," Cleve stated. To which Odell quipped quickly, "Yo' ass is old. I'm still layin' mo' pipe than a plumber! Shit, young hoe was here da' udda day talkin' 'bout, "Daddy, you sure know how to lay pipe." Cleve started laughing as Odell continued his fabrication, "I knew she wasn't lying but I had to set the hoe straight so I said, 'Bitch get in dere and make me some biscuits.'" Cleve doubled over in laughter, "Man, ain't nobody made yo' ass no damn biscuits!"

"Shit! Yea, she did! Den she po'ed honey on her chest and said, 'Lick it like you like it!' Then I had to slap the hoe 'cause I ain't 'bout to have no broad tellin' me what to do. Shit, what da fuck I look like? Dudley Do-Right or something?"

Cleveland cut him off before he could continue his fantastic extrapolation, "Dell man, I gots to push on. Me and Elaine, got plans." Odell shouted, "Plans?!" Yeah, yo' ass is still whipped. But it ain't too late to gets yo' side piece action going. Shit, you could use some biscuits in yo' life!"

As Cleve headed to his work van, he reflected on the sad, delusional life of his friend. They had been classmates in high school and worked on the assembly line together, but Cleve realized that he didn't really know Odell at all. He knew

Odell's blustery facade and pimp delusions, but today, it was as if Cleve was really seeing Odell for the first time. After backing out of the driveway and turning to head down the street, Cleve honked the horn and raised a fist at his friend. Odell was out of breath after struggling up the steps. His wave was weak as he held the porch railing with his other hand before falling back into a worn lawn chair. He would sit in that chair for hours, dipping and spitting snuff, as his health withered away. "He was alive," Cleve thought, "but he sure ain't living."

22

WAKE UP, EVERYBODY

Harold Melvin & the Blue Notes

February 20, 2015

The winter weekend break was a welcome time for Joyce to catch-up on paperwork. She and Elaine spent a large part of the morning reviewing the instructional coaching notes Elaine had compiled for each teacher. These notes would evolve into recommendations on the teachers' upcoming evaluations.

Knowing that the busyness of the day could make them lose track of time, the ladies set an alarm for three o'clock. They planned to pick up the food they ordered by 3:30 and be at Joyce's house by four to watch *Real Talk Detroit*. Today's guests on *Real Talk* would be Emergency Manager Wellington Shelby and Ella Baker Academy Principal Reverend Amos Thigpen. The host of *Real Talk* was the suave-but-tough Chuck Randall, who was Detroit's version of the legendary Ed Bradley. Randall had a reputation for asking the questions most reporters were too modest to ask. Viewers knew Randall was going to go hard when he prefaced a question with "The people want to know."

For Joyce and Elaine, today's show presented an opportunity for schadenfreude. They were aware of Shelby's role in the investigation of their late friend, Francine. While learning of Francine's shenanigans was unsettling, the revelation of the school district's intent to make her the metaphorical deer carcass on the hood of their investigations into impropriety conjured strong feelings of spite and assurance that their foresight to leave the district years prior was astute.

Then there was Elaine's monumental contempt for Reverend Thigpen, which was more intense than Donald Trump's disdain for science. Thigpen fanned the flames of manufactured outrage that led to Elaine's resignation. With allegations of theft being cast on school administrators citywide, the public climate was ripe for deception. It was as if the mismanagement of others had provided a 9/11-type attack on the public trust and Thigpen campaigned to seize Elaine's non-existent weapons of mass destruction. It was a conniving ploy to remove Elaine and assume the helm of power at Ella Baker Academy.

To those who didn't know better, it appeared that Thigpen's antics were reflective of a sincere commitment to the community. Chuck Randall was going to expose the truth.

Randall: Good afternoon and welcome to another episode of Real Talk Detroit, where we ask the questions you want to ask so that we can get the answers we deserve. Today's guests are two gentlemen at the forefront of the battleground of local public education: Detroit Public Schools' Interim Emergency Manager, Wellington Shelby, and Ella Baker Academy Principal, as well as Educational Acceleration Association School Reform District representative, Reverend Amos Thigpen. Gentlemen, is it true that neither of you has ever taught in a classroom or received any kind of administrative training?

Thigpen: I resent the insinuation. Since I received my calling to the ministry nearly forty years ago, I have been fully invested in the Lord's work. I...

Randall: Did that calling include any school teacher or administration experience, or was it more of an osmosis type of educational leadership enlightenment?

Thigpen recoiled in disgust and began plotting how he would walk off the stage to avoid being embarrassed.

Randall: While the Reverend recalls his formal training, we will ask Mr. Shelby about the progress of the #DPScomeback social media campaign. Is it positively telling our story?

Shelby: Thank you Mr. Randall…

Randall: Please call me Chuck.

Shelby: Well, thank you, Chuck. Our social media strategy has been an astounding success! On Twitter alone, we have had over a million tweets and retweets sharing the good news about DPS.

Randall: Mr. Manager, those numbers are impressive, but the tweets themselves are a bit revealing. For example, the picture of you ignoring a parent has been retweeted three thousand times. Or how about another tweet with over a thousand retweets from the Power to the People Project that says: "The DPS budget has consistently been in the red since the state took over. Restore local leadership." Or this frequently retweeted tweet from the Fact Check Consortium: "Despite the emergency manager's fiscal responsibility, the DPS deficits have multiplied and enrollment is plummeting."

Shelby: Chuck, our office has been working diligently to provide direct responses to inquiries such as these. I have the utmost faith in our team's ability to provide clarity where there is confusion.

Randall: Mr. Manager, the people need clarity. Beginning with the fact that an appointee over whom we had no say in appointing and who lacks educational experience or training is given command of an educational system that prioritizes finances over learning and instruction. Then this same overseer adds that employees of the educational system are devoting their time to addressing social media posts. Mr. Manager, the people want to know when will the education of our children will be a priority.

Elaine shouted, "Amen," as she and Joyce high-fived each other.

Thigpen: Chuck, it seems you have an axe to grind. The Bible warns us of your kind.

Randall: My job is to be a megaphone, amplifying the concerns of the people. Your job is to educate our children. And for you in particular, the people want to know about the witch hunt you led against former principal Elaine Robeson? The people cannot understand how she led one of the best schools in the city and was proven innocent of all allegations but was subjected to the board's acting upon your seemingly personal vendetta. Is this really God's work or that of an opportunist currying favor with the establishment?

With that, Thigpen stood up so abruptly that his chair toppled backwards, snatched the microphone from his lapel, and stormed off-stage. He could be heard shouting, "My God will not be mocked!" as he departed the set.

Randall looked into the camera with an "oh-boy" expression before turning back to Shelby, who was visibly rattled with sweat forming on his brow.

Randall: Is Reverend Thigpen your confidante or is he a stooge strategically placed by the governor to keep tabs on you?

Shelby: Reverend Thigpen is a steward of the community's interests.

Randall: And you know this how?

Shelby: He is a pastor and a man of God.

Randall: Self-proclaimed.

Shelby: Chuck, you should really do your homework. Everyone knows that Ella Baker Academy is what it is due to the stellar leadership of its school board. Reverend Thigpen has been essential to their success.

Randall: Our homework reveals that since the Thigpen-led coup, enrollment at Baker has declined substantially. They currently have less than a third of the students they had when Principal Robeson was leading the school. Is this the type of coaching you're getting from Thigpen? How to disservice a community and malign their servant leaders in an effort to pad your resume?

Shelby: I am an independent thinker who bounces ideas off of Reverend Thigpen, a minister of good counsel. I wake up every morning thinking of ways to best serve the children of Detroit.

Randall: Was that rehearsed?

Shelby: Is it your intent to shame me or will I have a chance to share the good news about Detroit Public Schools?

Randall: Please tell us the good news about student achievement, school safety, and teacher morale.

Shelby: The students of Detroit Public Schools are resilient. They have overcome more obstacles in their academic journey than most of us have ever faced. Despite overspending by previous leaders, fraud and larceny by former principals, and occasionally having to share their desks with other anxious learners, our kids are learning, striving, and growing.

Randall: Can you be more specific?

Shelby: Sure, Chuck. Here's a little-known fact: the number of student absences has decreased in each of the last five years. In fact, student attendance increased by 20% this past January compared to the previous January.

Randall: That sounds good, but the people wonder if the fact that there are seven thousand fewer students in the district than last year is the core of that potentially misleading data you shared. In fact, the Educational Acceleration Association School Reform District has taken over fifteen schools because student achievement has been so consistently low.

Shelby: The Educational Acceleration Association School Reform District is an olive branch from Lansing to help rehabilitate the inadequacies of challenged schools.

Randall: Are you sure it is not a conduit to reroute resources away from Detroit?

Shelby: That is not the intent of our governor.

Randall: The same governor who willfully ignored the toxic levels of lead in Flint's water? The people find it hard to imagine him considering what's best for our students.

Shelby: Chuck, you REALLY should do your homework. You will learn more about the DPS comeback!

Randall: Thank you, Mr. Manager. I'm afraid I have already done more homework than you, but you are responsible for salvaging our district. God help us.

Join us next week as we engage in Real Talk with local activists who are working to end youth violence.

"Chuck knows he can be a hard-ass, but I like him," Joyce stated as she turned down the volume.

"Yeah, ole Reverend Charlatan couldn't take the heat, so he got the hell out of the kitchen!" Elaine added, prompting them to erupt in laughter. Joyce mimicked Thigpen, "My God will not be mocked!" They laughed harder. Moments after the laughter subsided, Elaine wondered aloud, "Do you think things will get any better?" A rhetorical question that stirred the sad insecurities about the unlikeliness of their hopes.

23

AIN'T UNDERSTANDING MELLOW

Jerry Butler & Brenda Lee Eager

February 24, 2015

W ith the erect posture of a confident student who prepared all night for their book report, Elaine began sharing what she learned about Cleveland's mother.

"Josephine Robeson was a descendant of the Black Seminoles of Florida. She studied at Edward Waters College and became a teacher to the children of sharecroppers. In this role, she met Willie Robeson. As a teacher, she taught her husband to read. Also, most of Cleveland's sweetest childhood memories involve his mother reading to him and Columbus." Elaine looked at Cleve for confirmation that she was correct in her retelling. She continued, "Cleveland now knows but didn't quite recognize then that his mother could not get a teaching job in Detroit. As a child, he recognized a type of sadness gradually taking over his mother, who was very discontented at only being allowed to be a domestic." Cleveland nodded with additional consent. "Cleveland wonders if his mother's dismissive comments about her 'sugar acting up' was indicative of undiagnosed diabetes, or maybe if she had been diagnosed, she didn't share it with the boys. The increasing frequency of swelling in parts of her body preceded her transition."

Elaine swallowed hard, "Cleveland discovered his dead mother. He assumed she was getting dressed for an evening shift cleaning the hospital. She was slumped over on the floor with one shoe in hand and the other on her foot. She was pronounced dead at the hospital where she should have been working that evening." The trio permitted a moment of silence as Cleve bit his lip and hung his head. Elaine then added, "I thought it was worth noting that Cleve did not initially share his discovery with his brother. Columbus, who had begun pushing the limits of his mother's authority, did not arrive home until after Cleveland had returned from the hospital.

The silence returned for what felt like hours but was only a smattering of minutes. It was very apparent that Cleve was holding back his tears as he turned away and held his chin up. After the second wave of sadness spasms shook his body, Elaine hugged him from behind and pulled him close.

Observing this confirmed for Dr. Daniels that Cleveland had never fully shared the stories about either of his parents' deaths. She was sure that his nondisclosure was not borne of deceitful concealment but of emotional suppression and an unwillingness to revisit painful memories. As he cried, he continued covering his face and muttering, "I'm alright."

He had learned to coexist with pain. Dr. Daniels was hopeful that with Elaine's help, they could help him reach a peaceful resolution.

∿

STOKELY WAS MILDLY SURPRISED BY PHOENIX'S REQUEST THAT he accompany her and her mother to the funeral. He was more than willing, but had no idea how to offer his support. When Phoenix blurted the request over a short phone call, he thought of his father's palm tree swaying analogy and agreed to go along. Once Phoenix shared the details, she concluded the conversation in an abrupt manner.

Now as he pushed the cart containing all their luggage toward the airport rental car space, he figured that he would not only be a supportive chauffeur but an emotional safety net for the next few days.

After loading their bags into the trunk of a Lincoln sedan, Stokely got in the driver's seat and asked, "Where would y'all like to eat?" Denise replied, "Somewhere local." Phoenix had googled some soul food restaurants on her phone and added, "How does Big Mama's Soul Food sound? Stokely quickly replied, "Sounds like we're on our way! What's the address?"

"I FIGURED TALKIN' 'BOUT IT WASN'T GONNA CHANGE NUTHIN', so I just kinda put those memories way on the back burner of my mind," Cleve admitted sadly. "It wasn't no secret or nuthin', I just didn't want to remember what happened." He exhaled deeply.

"Cleveland, you've been repeatedly and significantly traumatized. Talking about those memories will not change what happened, but it can change how you live with it."

Cleve stared at Dr. Daniels while processing what she said. Then he added, with a twinge of sarcasm, "So we're letting air out some balloons, hunh?" The ladies laughed cautiously before Dr. Daniels added, "Yeah, we're on our way." She decided to push. "Why don't you want to cry about it?" Cleve looked surprised by the question. He shrugged his shoulders upward and replied, "All this carrying on, it just feels so unnatural."

"That's exactly the point," Dr. Daniels responded. "You have been living with traumatic soul burdens for most of your life—which were certainly not your fault, but have become burdens that you've become accustomed to living with. But here's the thing: you don't have to continue living with them. Look Cleveland, maybe you're tired of my account deductions and balloon metaphors, but I've got one more for you to illustrate what can happen as you unburden your soul."

He rolled his eyes while replying, "Alright Doc, lay it on me."

"How much air pressure is in the tires on a car?"

Cleve was confused but replied, "Well now, depending on the tire and the size of the car..." Elaine shot him a glance that conveyed that he was being too technical. He resumed, "But yeah, you know, the standard American truck tire should have 35 pounds of air pressure. But you wanna be…"

Dr. Daniels cut him off, "Can the tire roll with just 20 pounds of pressure?"

Cleve was puzzled, "Yeah, but you don't want to do that. See, you could end up damaging your rims. Shit, if you hit one of them East side potholes, you might fuck up your axle. Nawl, don't fuck around with 20 pounds; you'd be burning up all your gas and..."

The lightbulb of awareness came on as Cleve looked at each woman who stared back at him with knowing expressions. He nodded his head, "yes," and stated, "So yeah, them trauma burdens will have your tires damn near flat. We wanna keep our tires at the right pressure, know what I mean?" Everyone laughed.

Dr. Daniels turned up the pressure a little more, "So you never knew that your mother was suffering?" Cleve shook his head, "No." Dr. Daniels went on, "Which isn't unusual. There is a chance she did not fully know either. Or perhaps, circumstances may have caused her to feel hopeless. But the fact is she cared for you two as best she could and as long as she could." Cleve managed a small smile.

"Cleveland, does your family know your health situation?" Cleve clapped, pointed at Dr. Daniels, and exclaimed, "YES! Song has been going with me to my appointments. Plus, me and 'Laine been skating nearly every Friday night for a couple of months, and we even go walking pretty regularly."

"That sounds like you're doing something about your blood pressure, and I commend you for being proactive about it. This therapy can take your proactivity a step further." Dr. Daniels leaned forward and said, "Are you ready to talk about Columbus?" Cleveland's shoulders slumped and he slowly shook his head, "No."

"Is it easier for you to tell Elaine and have her start the conversation when we meet again?" Cleve shook his head, "yes," like a shy school boy. "Great! That's our plan. Elaine, how do feel about it?"

Elaine was experiencing a confluence of pride, support, love, and sadness. She hadn't ever really known the depths of Cleve's trauma. She reflected on having articulated her feelings of abandonment and Cleve's listening with empathy. She recalled him overcoming the awkwardness of accompanying her on that spur-of-the-moment trip to Arkansas to confront her parents. In all his efforts to support her as she made peace with her past, Elaine now realized that he had not made peace with his own past. He had been masking or ignoring his pain, coping or driving with nearly flat tires. She was committed to helping him heal. "Sounds great to me! We'll be ready to share next week."

As they rose to leave, Cleve was the last to stand. He stood slowly and exhaled deeply. He looked back at the spot on the couch he was occupying and stared for a moment. It was as if he was leaving something behind.

MISSING YOU

Diana Ross

February 25, 2015
Nashville

They were seated in the front row: Tanya, Denise, Phoenix, and Stokely. They were the only African-Americans attending the service—unless someone wants to count the deceased, whose life didn't include any Black people beyond his wife. A man whose life had taken him from New Orleans to various points around the globe. A life that introduced him to many but permitted bonds with few. That dearth of bonds was apparent in the sparse collection of mourners gathered in the small funeral home chapel.

Perhaps this is what happens when one has lived a series of compartmentalized lives where the people over here do not know the people over there. Tanya, Oscar's wife, had only recently learned of one relative, an estranged daughter, through her own set of peculiar circumstances. Had it not been for the unraveling of Tanya's extramarital affair, she would have never learned of Oscar's daughter.

There was an abundance of flowers donated by an assortment of colleagues, investment partners, fellow board members, and other professional acquaintances. The service included several readings of resolutions that sounded like impressive formalities of insignificance. However, there did not seem to be anyone who could be considered a close friend. Tanya mused that perhaps she was Oscar's closest friend. An ironic feeling because "close" was not an adjective among the descriptions of their marriage. It was a minor relief to consider that Oscar may not have been close to anyone, and thus what they shared was the maximum of his capacity to be close. Probably so, but understanding that now was irrelevant.

Denise was stoically sad as she pondered that the bond she longed to share with her ex-husband was one that he was incapable of fulfilling. She reflected on the futility of her overtures to make something "click" in Oscar's emotions; efforts on her part to open the floodgates of affection for him. However, as she took in the setting and the distant interactions of those gathered, the notion that there were no floodgates to his emotions, or maybe if there were, Oscar would have had to have the willingness and the guidance of a professional to unlock them. It was sad to contemplate that a man of wealth and material trappings was so empty inside.

Phoenix was angry. All of her resentful feelings of aban- donment and imaginations of what she may have missed were bubbling in her spirit. She could not think of any reason why Oscar chose to leave her and her mother. She knew that she carried this anger and perhaps it displayed itself in her quick temper. The thought of her temper prompted an additional twitch of anger, which led to the squeezing of Stokely's hand. She turned to him as he was facing her with an expression of concern and compassion. Looking into his eyes prompted a spiritual cold bucket of water onto her campfire of resentment. She leaned her head over onto his shoulder and felt calm overcome her as he gently stroked the side of her face with his free hand. She wiggled a bit closer to him.

Stokely recalled his phone conversation with his mother, who shared that he had one job during this time of grief—care for Phoenix. "Be intentional, not overly dramatic, but emphasize the little things that show concern and support." The wisdom of his mother's advice was affirmed with the gentle bumping of Phoenix alongside him. He kissed the top of her head, and she clasped their joined hands with her free hand. Stokely looked at Oscar's body in the casket and felt pity. When he considered the father Cleve is to him and Song, as well as the husband he is to Elaine, Stokely considered that Oscar really missed the joy his family would have brought to his life. He also understood the void in Tanya's life that allowed their affair to happen. Perhaps she channeled emotions she wanted to share with her husband through him. Then Stokely pumped the brakes on those thoughts and reconciled that Tanya's reasons were neither here nor there and that they were certainly in the past. His present included this wonderfully smelling flower that was gripping his hand and leaning on his shoulder. Yep, he was going to willfully and dutifully follow his mother's advice.

The service was brief and impersonal. The minister delivering the eulogy didn't know Oscar, and his attempts at comfort felt perfunctory and hollow. Absent was the paradoxical sad delight of long-lost relatives embracing each other afterwards or chatter amongst old friends recalling the good times with the departed. Instead, Stokely overheard one man's phone call regarding tee time at the golf course. Phoenix observed how few of those gathered approached Tanya to offer condolences. Denise affirmed that as painful as the dissolution of her marriage had been, it had saved her from the joyless years that awaited had they remained together. Tanya began to exhale. She cried on the day of and in the days following Oscar's death. She had no more tears. She did have an inkling of laying down a burden, a premonition of freedom, a hope for the future. For her, resolution would be nearly complete with what she wanted to do next.

"Denise, would you mind if you and I had dinner?" Tanya inquired. Denise, who was pleasantly surprised by the invitation, answered, "Do you want to go now?"

Tanya exhaled slowly and replied without sarcasm, "Why not? It doesn't appear that we will miss anything."

The wives of Oscar Rousseau the Third joined hands and headed to the limousine. The cremation of Oscar's remains precluded a trip to the cemetery, and a repast was unnecessary for such a disconnected gathering of people. Denise waved to Phoenix and Stokely, "I'll catch up with you later!" as the limo driver opened the door for her and Tanya.

They returned the wave and headed toward the Lincoln. As they walked, Phoenix confided, "That was the most emotionless funeral I have ever been to." Stokely simply nodded his head in agreement. When he opened her door, she got on her tiptoes and kissed him. "Wow," he thought, "Where did that come from?"

He would soon find out.

CURIOUS

Midnight Star

February 25, 2015
Detroit

The deep-dish seafood pizza dinner at Pizza Papalis had been a pleasant treat, but the conversation afterwards while walking the streets of Greektown was the most rewarding and cathartic.

"How long do you plan on working with your dad?" Wes inquired.

Song sighed with a smile. "Until..." then she made an "on and on" gesture with her hand. "We're partners now, and it will be my business whenever, you know, that time comes."

"Oh."

"Guess how I'm going to grow it, though?"

"How?"

"I'm going to employ a team of female plumbers and electricians," Song stated with confidence.

"Hmmm, sounds like there is more to that idea. Go on, elaborate."

"Just think how many women forgo repairs or feel

uncomfortable when some strange man comes to do repairs in their home."

Wes paused to consider before adding, "Okay, yeah, when you put it like that. I can see that as a unique market."

Songhai nodded her head, "yes," as she continued, "It is an untapped market. In fact, those women make up the majority of our new clients because they trust me. So far, the revenue per job is smaller, yet the number of those small jobs has tripled. We're increasing our profit by doing more of those jobs, which puts less of a physical demand on my dad while helping me master the basics."

A sharp wind cut along Woodward Avenue as the couple approached Campus Martius. "Wow," Song marveled, "None of this was here before I got locked up." A realization that caused her to hang her head a bit. At first, Wes did not notice, as he shared, "Yeah, they are really building up Downtown. Even the Pistons are coming back to that new arena they're building down the street. You know, they're..." Then he noticed that Song had slowed their walking pace. He stopped and faced her.

"Songhai, you've already served the time. You don't have to continue to serve it again and again with regret."

She looked up with a morsel of hope. "I'm an ex-con plumber."

"You are a budding entrepreneur with an essential skill."

Another flicker of hope sparkled in her eye.

"Prison is hell. They tried to destroy my spirit."

"They failed, and you're stronger. Strong as hell to be exact."

"Look at this, my kid brother's buddy is trying to make me feel good."

Wes kissed her forehead, "We ain't kids no more. I'm a man, and hopefully, I can be your man."

Song looked into his eyes. Trust and hope were emotions

with which she had little experience outside of her family; however, those emotions converged as she stepped into Wes' embrace.

Nashville

It was all Denise could muster to not spit the wine out of her mouth in laughter after Tanya asked if she had ever found Oscar to be standoffish. She cupped one hand over her mouth and held up one finger with her other hand as she slowly swallowed.

"Tanya, I used to wonder whether standoffish was his middle name!"

They laughed, then Denise went on. "As far as I can tell, that emotional distance was always a part of who he was. But when we were dating and first married, it showed infrequently. In my youthful naivety, I saw it as just an occasional bad day." Tanya shook her head in agreement that the man Denise described sounded much like the man she married.

"But after the Persian Gulf War," Denise threw up her hands in exasperation as she explained, "Those occasional bad days became the norm. He wasn't physically or verbally abusive. But he was certainly detached." Denise reflected further, "When I picked him up from the airport after his last deployment, I had on my head-turning dress and my favorite perfume, and this idiot gave me a hug and a damn pat on the head!" Angry disappointment resurfaced with the memory. The attempt to mask that disappointment with laughter was betrayed by the pain in her eyes.

"He what?! Oh hell no!" Tanya responded, "I would have had to kick his ass!" Tanya responded.

"I should have, but instead I thought something was wrong with me. My fears made me assume there was someone else."

A silence hung between them. The notion of "someone else" prompted both women to think about Tanya and Stokely. Denise avoided the elephant in the room and resumed her description of Oscar. "Shortly thereafter, he continued to request, or at least be assigned to, different bases around the country without ever requesting the transfer of his family. It took me some time, but I got the message; he did not want to be a family." Denise sipped her wine and added, "Our marriage was annulled—like it never happened. My anger would not accept child support from someone so indifferent. Although I never spoke negatively to Phoenix about her dad, over time she developed her own feelings borne of abandonment and resentment."

Tanya seemed to share Denise's heartbreak. She commiserated, "I'm sorry you had to go through that. You and Phoenix certainly did not deserve it." Denise mouthed "Thank you" before finishing her wine. "What about how he treated you?"

Tanya sighed, "Weeeellllll" and let out a long exhale. "I hope this doesn't sound odd, yet somewhere along the way, I got the feeling that he was doing his best. He scripted our affection." Denise's expression formed a question mark. "I told you it was odd, but it's true. For example, he scheduled "sex" for every other Saturday." Denise's expression transformed into horror. Tanya nodded "yes" while continuing, "He even saved it on our iPhone calendars." Denise moved from horror to incredulity. "Yes, everything felt so thought out and so planned that our life felt regimented and impersonal." This time, Tanya sipped her wine. "It is from this space that I took the job with Chrysler, moved to Detroit, and eventually, well, you know, met Stokely."

"I understand. Stokely is a wonderful young man and I could see how he could fill that void Oscar created," that was as about as far as Denise wanted to venture into Tanya and

Stokely's story. Tanya picked up on the vibe and continued, "When Oscar found out, he was furious to say the least, but around the same time, I became aware of his health challenges."

"Is it true that Stokely performed CPR on him?" Denise asked for confirmation.

Tanya pursed her lips and said, "Yes, girl. My other man breathed life into my husband."

"Waiter!" Denise semi-shouted, causing the maitre d' to rush over. "We're going to need more wine!"

Detroit

After walking back to Wes' Jeep Grand Cherokee, Song revisited his pronouncement from earlier. "Are you serious about wanting to be in a relationship with me?"

"As serious as a heart attack."

"You know, I haven't been so lucky with boyfriends."

"Yeah, I used to be jealous of what's his face? I couldn't believe y'all were really a couple."

Song slumped a bit and said, "Talk about regrets."

"I would rather die than ever have you regret us being together."

Song smiled. Then she added, "Why are you playing with my emotions?"

Wes reached in his coat pocket for a letter he had written with his left hand in crayon. The letter read: "I like you. Do you like me?" It included two check boxes with accompanied by the words, yes or no.

Song giggled warmly, leaned across the seat and kissed Wes on the cheek. She followed the kiss with "Yes." Wes blushed deeply but tried to keep his composure. He pointed to the letter, "Nah, it ain't official 'til you put it on paper."

To which Song erupted in laughter, "Okay, okay, where are the crayons?"

"You mean you don't have your own?" They both laughed. Then Wes opened the arm rest and produced a box of eight. "What color would you like?"

"Orange!" she clapped excitedly. The warm brilliance of orange was a stark contrast to the drabness of prison. Song wanted a future of vibrant color and Wes was more than willing to be the Basquiat painting her dreams.

26

I NEVER LOVED A MAN THE WAY I LOVE YOU

Aretha Franklin

February 26, 2015
Nashville

Their cocktail of perspiration tasted sweet as Phoenix licked a bead of sweat from Stokely's chest while he slept. He often teased her about being his kitten, and tonight was confirmation of that fitting tease. She had never been a snuggler, but she was nestled so close to Stokely that whenever he rolled over, she rolled with him. In the course of their relationship, she had evolved to seamlessly switch between being the snuggler and the snugglee.

Within the course of a night, Stokely may shift from his right side to his back and occasionally to his left side. But when joined in bed by Phoenix, she is everywhere. Her frequent movements caused him to wonder how she gets any sleep. Her favorite bed maneuvering is awakening before him, sitting on her bottom beside him, and resting the soles of her feet on his abdomen. She likes the way his muscles feel beneath her feet. Their connecting bond seemed strengthened when she watches his chest rise and fall during a new day's dawn. She is comforted when he caresses her ankle and drowsily replies, "Good morning, Baby."

Her frequent repositioning had little to do with restlessness and more with her desire to be close to Stokely. Tonight, she could still smell the traces of the cologne he put on before the funeral. She cuddled closer and, though asleep, Stokely's arm reflectively pulled her closer. She promised to write an online journal and both commend and verify the urging that couples should sleep nude, which has been the icing on the cake of her relationship with Stokely. While sleeping nude eased the foreplay of lovemaking, the intimacy it provided seemed to be the glue of her relationship.

Before drifting asleep, she wondered if her parents shared this kind of companionship and if recapturing it was what kept her mother hoping for a reconnection. The thought of her mother made her ponder if she locked the door joining Stokely's hotel room with the room she shared with her mother. She contemplated getting up to check but had finally gotten into the perfect position, curve for curve, bend for bend, with the soles of her feet perfectly fitted aligned along the tops of his. She wasn't getting up. If mom saw them, she'd just see them. She already knew that Phoenix was certain of a future with Stokely, more of a certainty than Denise ever had with Oscar.

1990

Denise sat in the dark on the edge of their bed, seething in a combustible mix of anger and disappointment. Oscar lay asleep, snoring near the other edge of the bed. She was tired of being the initiator to a seldom responsive spouse. She was tired of attempting to fix some different part of herself in an effort to appease him. She was tired of conjuring another excuse for their toddler's inquiries about Oscar and his whereabouts. She imagined that decades ago, some women would have been content with a husband who provided a house, paid all the bills, and otherwise took care of all the inanimate things that make up a family. Those women would probably have been appalled at Denise's audacious dissatisfaction. But Denise knew that she deserved better.

On this night, she looked over her shoulder and was struck with the lightning bolt of certainty; she would be happier if they were apart. She swallowed a huge lump of acceptance. When she stood and caught a glimpse of her reflection in the mirror made visible by the moonlight, she acknowledged there was nothing more she could do to bridge the emotional separation in their union. He had to meet her somewhere, and as she looked again at the bed, she realized that he wouldn't.

She slipped each arm into her house robe, tied it tightly at the waist, and left their bedroom for the last time, closing the door behind her.

2015
Detroit

Elaine sat up, leaning on one elbow, and stated the obvious to Cleve, "It is different without the TV." Cleve shook his head in agreement. Earlier that day, they moved the television and the TV stand from their bedroom to the basement. In addition to opening space in their bedroom, it created space for a little night time conversation.

Elaine placed her palm on Cleve's chest, "Honey, I'm proud of you." Cleve turned to her in confusion. "A lot of men would never participate in therapy and I don't know why, but I'm glad you chose to." Cleve didn't know what to say. Elaine continued, "Also, I'm sorry for not really being there for you and what happened with your family. I just didn't even know, let alone... " Cleve placed a finger on her lips. Then he turned on his side, sat up, and leaned on his elbow. Facing each other, he said, "Nah, you ain't got to apologize for that. I ain't share it with you because I didn't know how. I wasn't trying to hide nothing, I just ain't really wanna go there again." Elaine placed her hand on his shoulder. "Daniels got a point about letting the air out of the balloons." Cleve chuckled. "I know she bet not come up wit' no more analogies or she gonna confuse the hell out of me." They both laughed.

"Do you feel any different?" Elaine inquired cautiously.

Cleve thought for a moment, "Yeah. I don't know if it's too early to tell, but for me, reflecting on how me and you done came through and how well things are going with Song —all that is helping me feel better." He paused before adding, "Plus my legs aren't as sore no more when we finish skating." Elaine chuckled, "Mine neither." Then she kissed Cleve, turned away from him, and backed into a spooning position. She reached for his hand and pulled it to her mouth to kiss, "Good night, Cleveland." He smiled in the dark, leaned forward to kiss her behind her earlobe, and replied, "Good night, Baby."

27

WAY DOWN IN THE HOLE

The Five Blind Boys of Alabama

February 27, 2015

I t was 7:45 in the morning, and Wellington Shelby could not figure out why Reverend Thigpen was exiting the administration building. He thought it unusual but decided against calling out to the Reverend, figuring that he did not have time for a drawn-out conversation. He started thinking of what he wanted to accomplish this morning and pushed the odd occurrence to the corners of his mind.

The second oddity was that the receptionist had not arrived. He promised himself he would learn her name soon enough. He was making that mental note when he pushed open the doors to the conference room to which his office was adjacent. Seated at the conference room table were an attorney and two representatives from the governor's office. Their solemn expressions prefaced the bad news they had come to share.

"Good morning!" Shelby said it with a glee that belied his concern. A taciturn official responded with, "Please have a seat, Mr. Shelby. There are urgent legal matters that we must discuss with you."

"Legal matters? I don't understand."

"Which is why you should have a seat," the attorney forcefully inserted.

Shelby placed his bagel and latte on the table and pulled back the chair opposite the trio. When he sat, he suppressed feelings of fear and confusion. The attorney did not delay, "Since shredding legal contracts on television and halting payments to several vendors, you have opened the district to liabilities and additional bad press."

Shelby retorted, "As the emergency manager, I have the right to cancel contracts." To which the attorney sarcastically replied, "As the interim, you have the responsibility to recommend contractual revisions to our office, where we will deal with the particulars."

"How can I serve the district if my actions have to be cleared by the governor's office?" Shelby shouted, with increasing confusion and anger.

The third member of the trio spoke up, "Mr. Shelby, your role is ceremonial. Consider it as optical window dressing for the people of Detroit. The governor's office welds the decision-making power."

Shelby was confused. He had really believed he was in charge.

The attorney added, "We have a prepared statement that will be announced at a 9:00 am press conference. You will be placed on administrative leave for two weeks. During this time, you are advised against making any public announcements. I would strongly suggest that you leave right now and await a call from our office sometime next week."

Shelby would never understand that while he was parading his brand around the city, the choice of cutting off vendors who were longtime donors to the governor expedited the brevity of his turn at the helm of leadership. No, he would never see that truth as he foolishly believed that those politicians were his friends.

The 9:00 a.m. press conference featured one person: the Reverend Amos Thigpen. He began the session in a eulogistic tone. He tapped the microphone, "Is this microphone on? It is? Okay..." he straightened his lapels, made a little side-to-side motion with his head, and began. "Good morning Detroit, parents and students of Detroit Public Schools. It is with great sadness that I address you this fine morning. As you are well aware, our public school system is facing many obstacles—some that we will overcome, and others that require a doubling-down of our efforts. Nonetheless, I stand before you with the heartbreaking news that..." He stiffened his bottom lip and pretended to catch a tear from his eye. "Our friend and trusted leader, Mr. Wellington Shelby, has been placed on administrative leave." Thigpen lifted his head to the sky, closed his eyes, and whispered a plea, "Lawd Gawd have mercy!" He regrouped and looked into the camera, "While his intentions were in the right place, securing minority contractors to service our needs, his judgement and actions appear compromised."

With that, he unveiled a poster-sized grainy photo taken from a security camera. The unflattering photo was of Songhai Robeson. "Mr. Shelby's greatest lapse in judgment was attempting to replace vetted contractors with notorious ex-convicts." Thigpen bowed his head and shook it from side-to-side. "But Detroit, we cannot allow his misjudgment, his mistake, his dalliances with convicts to deter us from our mission to provide the best education for our children. I simply could not stand by idly while he led us down this path to perdition. Someone has to take a stand and say, 'ENOUGH!'" He pounded his fist on the podium. He regained his composure and continued, "The governor has requested that I steer our ship through these treacherous seas of uncertainty to the safe harbors of student achievement and stable leadership." He paused so that the gravity of what he was saying could sink-in. He resumed with solemn modesty, "Whether it is the students of Ella Baker Academy, the Educational Acceleration Association School Reform District, or Detroit Public Schools, I am a leader whose heart is guided by God and whose commitment is to our community. I pledge to work steadfastly with the Detroit Public Schools staff and do my best to keep our children away from convicts like this!" He slapped his palm against the poster board so hard that it overturned off of the dais.

The press conference was scheduled to be the story for the lunchtime news broadcasts on all the major stations.

KEEP YA HEAD UP

2Pac

February 27, 2015

Songhai answered the phone to hear Elaine bellow, "Song! Put yo' Daddy on the phone!" Cleve and Song were laying on their backs underneath a kitchen sink. The home owner had previously hired some jackleg plumber who, for a case of beer, commenced to completely fuck up their pipes. Song was removing the pipes as Cleve worked the wrench. When she handed him the phone, with a puzzled look on her face, they both slid out of the cabinets and sat up. Cleve wiped his hands on his pants before taking the phone from Song.

Fractions of a second after he said, "Yeah, go on" into the receiver, Elaine erupted. "That gobble necked son-of-a-bitch got my baby all on the news calling her a convict!" Cleve was startled and confused. "Hold on now 'Laine. Run that by me again. Say what now?"

With angry deliberation, Elaine shouted, "That two-faced phony-ass alleged man of God is up on this TV talking about Songhai!" Cleve attempted to cover the receiver and asked the home owner, "Can you turn on the news, right quick?"

From the kitchen table, the home owner extended the remote towards the TV and changed it from Steve Harvey's *Family Feud* to a local news station. "Yeah, that's fine. Thanks." Then he spoke into the phone, "What channel you watching, 'Laine?"

She responded, "I'm watching four, so y'all try seven. They might not have run the story yet."

"Okay, we watching seven now. Wait a minute, hold up." He gestured for the home owner to turn up the volume and waved for Song to pay attention. Channel Seven was just beginning to air the clip from the press conference. Songhai was embarrassed to tears when she saw the blown-up poster board from her visit to McKenny Elementary. Being referred to as a convict on television was shamefully heartbreaking.

When water droplets land on a hot skillet, they sizzle before evaporating, Cleveland was so hot with rage that water droplets would evaporate in proximity to him. They would not land on his head nor sizzle; he was so angry that the air around him turned to steam.

The homeowner pointed his remote at Song, then back at the TV, and said, "That's you?"

Song left the room, went outside, and headed to the van. Thankfully, Cleve did not see Reverend Thigpen knock the board over, or he would have erupted like Krakatoa. Instead, he followed his daughter out the door after dropping the phone to the floor.

Neither a blizzard nor a snowstorm could have cooled Cleve's anger as quickly as the necessity of tending to his daughter's pain. He grabbed her from behind and wrapped her in a protective embrace. "Alright now, Daddy's gonna handle this. Just let it out. I'm gonna take care of it. You hear me? Daddy is gonna straighten it out." He rocked her slowly from side-to-side as she sobbed, "Why are they doing this? I did the time. Daddy, I did the time."

After a few minutes, Cleveland directed his daughter, "Now go on and wait in the van. I'll be out shortly." As Songhai consented, Cleveland re-entered the home. The homeowner had gathered their tools into a pile and told Cleve, "Y'all got to get out of here. I don't allow no criminals in my home." Cleve's expression was so fierce that the home owner pulled out a fifty dollar bill to defuse the tension before adding, "That's for the little work y'all started."

Cleve took the fifty in his hand, looked at the customer, and then balled the bill in his fist and threw it in the man's face. He gathered the tools and responded with, "Fuck you and your raggedy-assed kitchen." He scooped up his phone to find that Elaine was still holding the line. He flung the tool belt over his shoulder, headed toward the door, and asked for Elaine.

She responded defiantly, "That asshole! He's going to pay for hurting my baby!" Cleveland could hear the sniffling of Elaine's angry tears. "Are y'all done with the job?" Cleveland responded, "Yeah, 'Laine we done for the day. We 'bout to head on to the house." Between sniffles, she added, "Just c'mon home. Bring my baby home."

29

PAPA DON'T TAKE NO MESS

James Brown

March 1, 2015

The glistening sheet of black ice that topped the streets of Detroit encouraged a number of regular churchgoers to attend Bedside Baptist with their favorite preacher via television or the internet. However, despite this morning's being the first live broadcast via social media, the members of Reverend Thigpen's church arrived as an enthusiastic throng of supporters riding the wave of their pastor's growing local notoriety.

Typically, it goes unsaid, yet a number of church attendees participate in a one-upmanship game of "My Pastor Is Better Than Yours." Usually, it's a veiled comparison, modestly couched within the spoken question of "What church do you attend?" The ensuing silence is the questioner calculating whether they had heard of the church, with a faint acknowledging expression accompanied by the inquiry, "Is that Pastor So and So's church?" Based on one's response, there is an acceptance comparable to being invited to the popular kids' table in a middle school cafeteria.

Reverend Thigpen's church was far from the most popular, but it was experiencing a surge of popularity. Perhaps it is odd to discuss churches and popularity, but the discussion incorporates the social interactions that occur alongside the communes with Jesus. Indeed, there are some churches whose emphasis on social influences exceeds their rapport with Jesus, and a few other churches whose commitment to collecting offerings exceeds their commitment to serving the community. Reverend Thigpen's church was somewhere in the middle, trudging toward insignificance as his ministry became less and less about Jesus and more and more about Amos Thigpen.

ELAINE WAS FRIGHTENED. HER MAMA BEAR INSTINCTS HAD been lit aflame by Thigpen's press conference. The most benevolent description of her history with him could only be described as acrimonious. She saw through his bluster, threats, and pronouncements of what the Lord revealed to only him and recognized an insecure, opportunistic narcissist who preyed on broken spirits with promises of divine protection. Frequently, he implied but never stated explicitly how one's divine protection was in correlation to their offerings and tithes.

Elaine saw through that. Thigpen knew that she saw through him and thus was committed to creating distractions between them so that others could not see the truth she saw. She was also pretty sure that his penchant for distraction probably did not allow him to connect with the woman he shamed during the press conference as the daughter of the principal he forced to walk the plank into an ocean of public skepticism. He was too self-centered to care about who he hurt as long as his big-ass head was on television.

None of her simmering spite answered why Cleveland

had arisen early, shined his shoes, ironed his shirt, shaved, and put on a suit and tie. She wondered, of all the Sundays, why was he going to church today? Was she sure he was going to church? His energy was so cold and detached, it seemed he was oblivious to her presence. She followed him from the bedroom as he checked his watch and grabbed the keys to their Cadillac DTS. At no point during the morning did he acknowledge her. He was laser-focused.

While others drove with caution, Cleveland maneuvered the DTS with ease. He made nearly every green light, safely swerved around potholes, and neared Thigpen's church in thirty minutes. He eased the Cadillac into a parking space along the residential street about fifty yards south of the church. He could hear the winding down of the choir and the organ as he strode slowly along the sidewalk toward the steeple.

Reverend Thigpen deliberately kept the pre-sermon formalities brief with a sensitivity to the ongoing live social media feed. He imagined a multitude of unchurched viewers tuning in for the first time, and he wanted dearly to get to the meat of the message, believing that would be the best way to maintain their attention. After asking the congregation to turn their bibles to Genesis 22: 9-13, he began reading:

> 9 *When they reached the place God had told him about, Abraham built an altar there and arranged the wood on it. He bound his son Isaac and laid him on the altar, on top of the wood.*
> 10 *Then he reached out his hand and took the knife to slay his son.*
> 11 *But the angel of the Lord called out to him from heaven, "Abraham! Abraham!" "Here I am," he replied.*
> 12 *"Do not lay a hand on the boy," he said. "Do not*

do anything to him. Now I know that you fear
God, because you have not withheld from me
your son, your only son."

13 *Abraham looked up and there in a thicket he saw*
a ram caught by its horns. He went over and
took the ram and sacrificed it as a burnt offering
instead of his son.

"May the Lord add a blessing for the reading of his word." Thigpen cleared his throat before proceeding. "The Bible reminds us that our God will provide when we are faced with our greatest fears. In the last few years, our community, and specifically our educational system, have drawn closer and closer to our greatest fear of miseducated and undereducated children. We've trusted in God as we've laid our children, our hopes, and our dreams on the altar as our God called out, 'Abraham!' You see, when you're in harmony, in tune, and in sync with the almighty, he only has to call ya once, 'Abraham!' Sometimes that call gets personal. It was for me. I was approaching the altar, afraid for our children, and God said, 'Amos!'"

Someone shouted, "Alright now, Pastor! Take yo' time!"

With that encouragement, he stepped around the pulpit with his stomach jutted out, chest full of self-importance, and an inclination toward spinning the Sunday sermon into a self-aggrandizing political diatribe.

The usher had intended to extend his hand to indicate that there would be no walking in the aisle; however, the threat emanating from Cleveland's glare prompted the usher to pull his arm back and pretend he was engrossed in the sermon. Thigpen's strut across the pulpit would make popular television evangelists marvel at how their style had been co-opted, even down to the cordless microphone affixed to the suit lapel.

Cleveland was mid-sanctuary when Thigpen saw a man proceeding down the center aisle. Thigpen assumed the man wanted to be closer to the front, and to an extent, he was right. "Brothers, sisters, fathers, and mothers, our lives have continuously proven how our God works in a mighty and often mysterious way!" He paused while realizing that the man was not taking a seat in the front pew. Was he approaching the altar? "Yes, my brother, heed the Lord's call," was Thigpen's attempt to make sense of the situation. The Call to Christ had not been issued. Where were the ushers? This interruption insured that he would attend the next usher's meeting, where he was certainly going to light a fire under their asses.

The deacons exchanged curious glances. None of them recognized the man and were either shocked at what appeared to be happening or assumed someone else would redirect the man to his seat. Viewers of the social media feed had questions about the man who entered their screen view of the pulpit.

All of their curiosities were quelled as Cleveland gripped the front of Thigen's suit and lifted him from the ground. In a low and sinister snarl captured by the microphone, Thigpen and the parishioners clearly heard Cleve declare, "Muthafucka you ain't got nair 'nuther chance to hurt my family. Because I will have my foot so far up yo' ass not even Jesus will save you." Cleveland shook Reverend Thigpen twice, as if he were an oversized rag doll, and tossed him to the floor. As he turned to face the stunned audience, he adjusted his suit jacket, straightened his tie, and walked down the center aisle. From the collective hush of surprise, murmurs and giggles arose only after Cleveland passed. Those whom he had yet to pass remained solemn in their disposition, as they didn't want any part of the ass-whippings Cleveland seemed willing to share.

The social media audience had a different response. A number of viewers with technical savvy were able to record the incident and forward a clip of the confrontation to their friends. Some even made short video clips with interlaced clips from various Samuel Jackson movies for additional laughs. The snarkiest among them tweeted the clip with an appropriate hashtag, #DPScomeback.

Cleveland drove home in calm silence, oblivious to his burgeoning fifteen minutes of viral internet fame.

30

WHATCHA SEE IS WHATCHA GET

The Dramatics

March 3, 2015

"**I** saw you..."

Those were the words Songhai's parole officer spoke before looking down into her pile of papers. Maureen Porter was an overwhelmed public servant. When she began this job, she thought she would be a catalyst for change in the lives of recent parolees. Overtime, she became a callous-hearted, bureaucratic paper pusher, doing the bare minimum not because she did not care but because the volume of her work wouldn't allow her to care. This survivalist ambivalence would not allow her to see the impact her words had on the parolee seated across from her.

Which is good because Songhai assumed Porter's comment was in reference to Reverend Thigpen's press conference. She was prepared to explain and defend herself; however, her view of the top of Maureen's head gave her pause. It made her wonder if Maureen saw her at all. But what Songhai had taken for a period ending a sentence, should have been heard as a comma followed by a discomforting silent pause before Maureen resumed. " ... started working with your father at, um, yes — Robeson Plumbing. Are you still employed with Robeson?"

"Yes."

"Good, we like it when parolees can maintain employment. How about your residence?"

"I am still living with my parents."

"How much are you paying for rent?"

"My parents are not charging me rent. They want me there."

"When were you—wait, what? Did you say they 'want you there?'" This confusion caused Maureen to look up for the first time and make eye contact with Songhai.

"Yes."

"Well, that's good," she smiled briefly before handing Songhai a small container. "Here, take this, write your name on the side, and after you fill it up, just set it over there." She pointed to a shelf just behind her desk. "And we should see each other again in two months. Do you think you'll still be employed?"

"Yes."

"That's good. Keep up the good work, sweetie," said Maureen as she stamped some papers and placed them in a bin on her desk. As Songhai walked slowly over to the bathroom, she looked back at her parole officer and wondered if all of this was necessary and if it even mattered. She then shrugged with the thought that Maureen's indifference told her that not everyone saw or even cared about Reverend Thigpen's campaign of self-importance or its casualties. Most people are consumed with their own lives, trying to make it from one day to the next.

~

"I SAW YOU," CHUCKLED DR. DANIELS, WHICH IN TURN CAUSED Elaine to laugh a bit, before Cleve looked at both of them and joined in with his own self-depreciating laughter. As the chuckles subsided, Dr. Daniels began, "I saw the press conference and was preparing to talk about it, but," she giggled, "then social media showed me you took matters into your own hands." They all laughed at the irony.

Cleveland was speechless. Jacking up Thigpen and tossing him to the floor was possibly one of the greatest stress relievers he had ever experienced. Hours afterwards, during Stokely and Phoenix's visit to the house, his son showed him how clips of the incident were making the rounds on social media. With each viewing, Elaine's emotions ranged from "Cleve, how could you?" to "Kick his ass, baby!" But Cleve laughed, albeit demurely, because in any other circumstances he would have been talking about cool heads prevailing, yet here he was tossing preachers around. Even Songhai managed a proud laugh at how her father chose to stand up for her.

Now in the therapist's office, Cleveland could not say he was proud of his behavior. But he could accept that it was necessary for him as a man, as a husband, and as a father.

"What was it that compelled you into action?" asked Dr. Daniels.

Cleveland shrugged. Elaine reached for his hand and took it in hers. When she looked into his eyes, he smiled before responding, "I was just tired." The ladies waited patiently as he conjured his ideas. "See, it is folks like him that keep us down." The ladies nodded in agreement. "Instead of him helping the youngster who was in over his head, Thigpen probably set him up for failure while acting like he was a friend." Cleve looked at his wife and said, "Instead of him helping Elaine, he did all he could to make her look bad while disrupting the education the students were receiving."

Cleveland's face contorted, "Then he gonna pull my baby into his mess? Calling her a convict on TV and she ain't got a damn thing to do with his bullshit?" Elaine patted his hand in an effort to quell his rising anger. He pointed empathically with his other hand, "See, that motherfucker was out of pocket with that shit. He…"

Elaine kissed his hand and got his attention. Some of the anger abated. Cleveland took a deep breath. While exhaling, the ladies noticed the patting of his foot. It was as if he were counting. The patting of his foot was in sequence with the clenching and re-clenching of his jaw.

Dr. Daniels snapped her fingers and said, "Cleveland, process it through. Do not bottle it up. Process it." She followed her directive with hand gestures that looked as if she were sliding something under a door.

"If I would've whooped his ass like I wanted to, I would have gone more than viral, I would have gotten arrested," Cleveland added.

"That's absolutely right! You made your point, quite convincingly I should say, without overdoing it or bottling it up further." Dr. Daniels smiled before adding, "Healing isn't always pretty, but every step is necessary. It was necessary for you to… um… communicate with the reverend. I really believe he got the message."

Elaine chuckled, "Oh, he got the message! That's for sure!" Her merriment eased what was left of Cleveland's anger. He began a smile of acceptance as he eyed the nonverbal encouragement of his wife and therapist.

WOMANIFESTO

Jill Scott

March 4, 2015
Albert Cleage Academy, Detroit

The core value of the non-profit organization, *Building Beautiful Daughters*, was to provide healthy, hands-on mentorship for Detroit's adolescent girls. Its founder, Phoenix Ellison, was a tireless advocate for girls. Her clientele included programs with middle schools, Girl Scout troops, and churches. Through her work, Phoenix hoped to create bridges to opportunities beyond her clients' current circumstances.

On this day, Phoenix had arranged for an all-middle school girls' assembly where she would lead a heartfelt conversation with Songhai Robeson. She believed that the students would relate to and feel inspired by Songhai. Phoenix also believed that the public platform could help Song get past being embarrassed by Reverend Thigpen and, more importantly, continue forgiving herself. Phoenix understood this whole endeavor as an idealistic long shot, but the principal's endorsement of the idea provided just enough affirmation to push ahead.

Songhai was so nervous that she was shaking as she sat in a chair on stage looking down at all those beautiful and eager faces. She was worried about whether whatever she shared would have any value to the girls. She was hopeful and even said a little prayer of good intention.

Phoenix sat in the chair facing her. They exchanged smiles that communicated warmth, support, and sisterhood; they were in this together. Phoenix winked and reached toward Song with a fist bump. Song returned the bump and smiled a hopeful smile.

> **Phoenix**: Young ladies of Cleage Academy, I want to introduce you to our featured guest, Ms. Songhai Robeson. Ms. Robeson is the co-owner of Robeson Plumbing. Prior to becoming a plumber, she served twenty years in prison for being an unwitting accomplice to a crime.

A collective gasp escaped the audience. The girls, ranging in age from eleven to fourteen, had already sized-up Songhai. They thought her to be pretty and assumed she was somebody famous, although they hadn't heard of her. They were a little confused by the idea of her being a plumber. Not one of the girls knew a female plumber, let alone one who owned a plumbing company. The image of this beautiful woman did not reconcile with what they thought a plumber should look like, and that sparked their curiosity about her. Curiosity that was heightened by the fact that she did not resemble anyone they knew who had recently been released from prison.

> **Phoenix**:I see your faces, and that tells me we should allow our guest to explain how she ended up in prison and, more

importantly, her process for forgiving herself and moving forward in life.

Songhai: Thank you all for being here. You are so beautiful. Looking at you reminds me of being younger with the world in front of me.

She sighed deeply and looked at Phoenix, who gave her a thumbs-up.

Songhai: I was a pretty good basketball player. I had been accepted into the college of my choice. My parents and little brother loved and supported me. I had it all.

She grimaced sorrowfully before continuing.

Songhai: Then I got a boyfriend, who wasn't even cute. He wasn't all that smart, and all he talked about was himself and hustling. I knew then that I should have never even given the time of day to someone like that. But, seeing the good in everyone, I foolishly believed that I could help him. Help him with exactly what? I don't know. I mean, have you ever come across a sad and abused puppy and wanted to care for it?

A number of the girls responded aloud, as others shook their heads in affirmation.

Songhai: Well, that's just about how it felt to become close with someone who I should have left alone.

Phoenix: Did anyone warn you about him?

Songhai: Well, my girlfriends were impressed with his jewelry and money, so they weren't any help. But my mother warned me without ever having met him. She felt that I was acting differently and avoiding bringing him around. She was right. Then she told me that if I was too ashamed to introduce him to the father, then I probably should not be seeing him.

All of the girls were leaning forward, listening.

Phoenix: I want to re-state what you just said because it's very important.

She turned to the audience.

Phoenix: If you are too ashamed to introduce the person you want to date to the people you trust, you probably should not be dating them. Turn to your neighbor and repeat that truth.

An audience of young teens repeating the truth she shared brought a smile to Song's face and loosened her up to talk more freely.

Phoenix: How exactly did you end up in prison?

Songhai: I was driving Man-Man and we stopped at a store. I stayed outside in the car while he went inside. While inside, he exchanged words with another customer, and that became a bigger confrontation. Man-Man shot the guy, who died some hours later. I was still outside, unaware of what had happened. When he returned to the car, he was talking tough like he always did. I did not know he had a gun, and I definitely did not know he had shot anyone. I drove away. That night, I was arrested at home. I was charged as an accomplice to the murder.

A sorrowful silence engulfed the audience.

Songhai: Then, like now, I was innocent. The lawyer tried to make it seemed as if we were Bonne & Clyde. Like I handed him the gun him. I was definitely naive, but an accomplice to murder? No, that was never me. But they still sentenced me to twenty-five years in prison.

Phoenix paused for a moment so the gravity of the statement could sink-in. The girls were so captivated that it was if they were all holding their breath. Before Phoenix could ask the next question, Songhai continued.

Songhai: I'm glad y'all are listening. Maybe some of you look at me now and think that prison isn't so bad. If you're thinking that, you are wrong, wrong, wrong! Prison is terrible. It crushes the spirit and usually makes people worse than they were when they arrived.

Songhai shook her head mournfully.

Songhai: Maybe you heard your mother or someone older say something like, 'It doesn't seem like it was that long ago.' That would be true outside of prison, but inside? Hearing people screaming through the night? People challenging your dignity every day? Seeing people give up the will to live? That time passes very slowly. Very, very slowly.

Phoenix: How did you make it through?

Songhai smiled.

Songhai: My family—they never stopped fighting. They visited consistently. My mother even wrote me long letters.

Telling me how beautiful I was and how where I was did not define who I was. She really would go on and on, writing about sometimes the littlest things like grocery shopping or sometimes big things like how she felt as a child. I read and re-read those letters over and over. Then I would re-write the letter, you know, copy it, just to feel closer to mom. Of course, I would write her back. I mean, seriously, I had plenty of time.

Phoenix's head nodding encouraged Song to continue.

Songhai: To y'all, your parents probably look the same. But let me tell you, think about them in five-year chunks. Like it's 2015, look at a picture from 2010 and then 2005 and you can see them slowly getting older. When my parents visited, I studied their faces, as if I was memorizing every smile, every wrinkle, and every expression. I felt like I was making a short movie of memories that I would replay in my mind when I was back in my cell. Then my little brother—wow— he grew from a boy to a man while I was inside. That really made me happy for him, but sadder for me because it made me think I was wasting so much time.

She paused before adding:

Songhai: Oh yeah, I tried this idea or practice my mother suggested in one of her letters. She recommended that I do at least one act of compassion for someone else each day. It could be a smile or a "thank you." But in a place where compassion is almost non-existent and where acts of compassion can be seen as a weakness, my mom's point was that thinking about others would mean I spent less time thinking about myself. While in prison, most of my self-thinking was of regret and anger. But in time, my small acts of compassion grew like a kind of flower in my spirit. That flower helped me survive and sort of sustained my hope that I would make it through.

In addition to listening to Song's story, the teachers also realized they did not have to tell any of the girls to put their phones away. They were captivated. Some other people were captivated also, a small group who slipped in the rear with visitor tags affixed to them. The names on the tags read: Mrs. Robeson, Mr. Robeson, Stokely, and Wes.

Phoenix: How did it feel to finally get released?

Songhai took a deep breath before answering.

Songhai: Actually, I had a couple of parole hearings where I was denied. I later learned that Man-Man had made parole before I did, which is all messed up. I mean, the murder gets released before the naive driver? That just doesn't make any sense. That last time, my parents got me a really good lawyer, and she and my brother accompanied me to the parole hearing, which finally went my way.

The entire audience clapped, causing Songhai to blush with gratitude. From her position on the stage, along with her nervousness, she couldn't see her personal support team in the back. Her mother was shedding proud tears as the men looked on with appreciation.

Phoenix: Share with us what you've been doing since you've been out with extra emphasis on your healing journey.

Songhai: Healing journey? Wow. Well, when I first got home, Stokely, my brother, and I surprised my parents. They did not know about the last parole hearing, so when we showed up at home... it was the best day of my life!

Phoenix: Give us the details.

Songhai: After we hugged and cried, we had pizza because my dad burned the dinner he left on the stove because we were so caught up.

That comment garnered plenty of laughs from the audience.

Songhai: But seriously, my mom took down my cornrows and washed my hair. Nothing says "home" more than that. Then, later, my dad and I talked about what's next. At first, I thought I'd just be helping him here and there. Within a couple of weeks, I came to enjoy the work, especially helping people with something so essential. More than that, though, is the time spent with my dad. I had never really considered myself a "Daddy's Girl," but I am living that truth now. You know what's funny? It's like at different points in our lives, one of our parents moves to the forefront. While I was in prison, my mom was... I can't say most important, that would be wrong. Let's just say she was my primary support. Now, I guess it's my dad's turn. I'm so blessed to have them. I truly wouldn't be here without their love and support.

Phoenix: Wow! Let's take questions from the audience. Does anyone have a question?

Tanesha jumped from her seat on the floor and vigorously waved her hand back and forth. When Phoenix acknowledged her, she blurted out her question before someone with a microphone could get to her. She screamed,

"Do you have a boyfriend?" A question that garnered more than a few equivalents to middle school "Amens."

> **Songhai** (blushing): Yes. He is wonderful. He really helps refocus me on where I am now and where we are growing. He consistently redirects me away from regret and beating myself up about the past. Sometimes, I swear he sounds just like my dad.

Numerous other hands shot up in the audience. Songhai answered each question graciously. To her family and friends, they could see in her countenance a type of refortification of her self-worth, her identity, and her healing. The assembly ran well over its allotted time as many of the girls wanted to hug and take pictures with her. The love was as overwhelming as it was necessary for Songhai's healing.

32

SEASONS CHANGE

Fertile Ground

March 11, 2015
Auburn Hills, MI

I t was 3:13 pm when the moving truck pulled out of the driveway of Tanya's small condominium. It was really happening. It being a reference to this new season of her life. Following Oscar's transition, she resigned from her job and listed her condo for sale. While her place was pleasant and warm, it was also sparsely furnished and decorated, as it was always intended to be a layover, not a destination.

After the end of her affair with Stokely and the dissolution of the lease on their shared apartment, Tanya found this condominium near her job. It was tangible evidence to both she and her husband that she was sincere in moving on from Stokely. A sincerity that was further reinforced by learning of Stokely's budding romance with her... dare she think it — her stepdaughter, Phoenix. But Tanya didn't need Phoenix to move on from Stokely; she had already done so. And now she was leaving Michigan to supervise the finalization of

Oscar's affairs and spend time at the Nashville estate she had previously treated as more of a resort than a home. With the completion of that thought, she said aloud, "I guess I'm headed home."

The honking from the car service that would drive her to the airport set her in motion. She grabbed her purse, her carry-on luggage, and an envelope made out to Denise Ellison. The envelope contained a check Tanya had written from her and Oscar's joint account. Neither Denise nor Phoenix were included in Oscar's will, yet Tanya hoped her letter and the check would provide some solace for the pain her husband imposed on his family.

Once she locked the door, she placed the keys in that special door-lock contraption real estate agents use. She walked to the mailbox on the curb, placed the envelope inside, and lifted the red flag to alert the mailman to pick-up. The chauffeur opened the door and reached for her bag as she did one final look-back at her haven during the season in a valley of transition. She smiled and shed a joyful tear. She was moving on; it was indeed, really happening.

Downtown Detroit

His car has not moved since he parked it that fateful morning after leaving the office.

His razor and other grooming essentials have gone unused.

What in the past had been a meticulously neat bachelor pad had become a disheveled den for a wounded soul that reeked of contained masculine funk.

The trash overflowed from the delivered takeout food boxes.

The dust on the window blinds was measurable due to their disuse.

With the exception of food deliveries, the front door was only opened once to retrieve the box of belongings that he left in the office along with a certified letter of termination.

His sole fleeting moment of euphoria came when viewing the viral clip of Reverend Thigpen being tossed to the floor. Wellington even doctored a clip to garner additional laughs under his burner Twitter account. Even so, his curiosity led him to the #DPScomeback links, and he was mortified at not only what the hashtag had become but also the wealth of information he did not know about the district. While he most certainly would never verbalize it to anyone, the time since his termination revealed just how far in over his head he was. Being honest with himself, he never imagined being in the position for long and intended to use it as a stepping-stone to something more prestigious. He believed that leading a large urban school district would set him apart from others. However, at no time did he fully grasp that leading such an organization required the selflessness and empathy that he lacked. Stupidly, he equated leadership with how things were presented as opposed to how they really were.

When considering how things looked, in the past few days, Wellington had taken to using a handheld mirror to see the reflection of his back whenever he was in the bathroom. No, he did not actually expect to see knife wounds, but the feeling of having been stabbed in the back was so pronounced in his thoughts that he would not have been surprised if the wounds and scars on his spirit manifested on his back. Plus, the idea that such wounds had been applied by an alleged "Man of God" was nearly vomit-inducing. How did he not see through that charade of support? That gotdamn son of a bitch had set him up!

Which led him to think, or better yet, conspire: how could he get them, or at least the Reverend, back? He figured he did not have the resources to expose the governor, so his little 140-character tweets were akin to throwing pebbles toward an aircraft carrier. Yeah, there is some catharsis in tossing the pebbles, but the thrower knows it will not amount to much. However, Reverend Thigpen? He was definitely within striking distance of a retaliatory blow that would at the very least embarrass him and possibly cost him one of the numerous jobs he holds. Yeah, Reverend Thigpen would be the target of Wellington's retribution. Retaliation is such an intriguingly sinister relief from embarrassment.

33

BROTHERS GONNA WORK IT OUT

Willie Hutch

March 17, 2015

"I'm ready to talk about Columbus," Cleveland declared after taking a seat. Dr. Daniels and Elaine exchanged glances of minor surprise and looked at him with a receptive happiness that communicated, "go ahead."

"I already talked about Bus's murder, so we don't need to relive that. So instead I want to talk about a good time, like when we got into the Motown Revue." The ladies leaned forward to listen more excitedly. "Now back in '64, we was trying to get a little stash in our slide, with me shining shoes and Bus pool sharking fools. All the effort we was putting into getting some cash made us really reluctant to spend it, if you know what I mean." The ladies agreed, with smiles.

"So looka here, me and Bus we millin' 'round the alley behind the Fox, you know, seeing if we could make a break for an unattended door or something, and wouldn't ya' know it, one of the Funk Brothers waved us over to help carry in the instruments." The joy from the memory was overtaking Cleveland's face as his smile grew wider with each sentence. "Now we done carried drums, trunks of clothes, and some other stuff, you know, in and out, in and out to the van in the alley and then backstage at the Fox. We done made a couple of trips, and when we brought in that last trunk, we was just kinda standin' 'round backstage—it was about two hours before the show. Didn't seem like none of the band was minding us, so we just kinda like slipped into the toilet and stayed there until we heard the music get going. The boom..." Cleve clapped his hands to illustrate the haste with which they moved. "We cut out them stalls and got us some seats near the front!" Cleveland began laughing. The ladies figured they missed the joke but laughed along simply because Cleve was laughing so heartily.

"Now I ain't neva been much of a dancer. You know, once I do my little two-step, I done exhausted my repertoire, but I know I can dance better than Smokey Robinson, that's for sure." These prompted more sincere laughs from the ladies. "Bus, that boy could cut a rug with the best of them. I mean, we twins and God was 'spose to split the gifts up fifty-fifty, but when it come to dancing God gave Bus ninety and gave me ten!" Cleve's merriment was priceless. "The Temptations were up there doing their steps and whatnot, and Bus over here in the side aisle doing their steps better than them!" Elaine could see that therapy must have been having some benefit because she had never heard this story before. Cleveland was really opening up.

"Later, we was at a greasy spoon over on Grand River, and Bus had this little honeydip, believing he actually did Motown's choreography. She was all-in too and gave him her number so they could get together and he could teach her his moves. We had to stick around long after she left, though, because the Motown story doesn't work if she sees us walking down Grand River on our way home." Cleve smiled.

"God, I miss my brother." The ladies exchanged knowing glances as Cleve basked in the warmth of memories.

STOKELY AND WES GOT TOGETHER FOR LUNCH, AND STOKELY cut to the chase, "You're really serious about my sister, hunh?" The question had more testosterone than Stokely usually uses with friends. In fact, once the words left his lips, he wished he could recall them and restate them with less edge. He and Wes were much too cool for Stokely's little brother bravado to come between them, and Stokely knew that Wes didn't deserve to be spoken to like some random dude. This was his old friend, his man, 100 grand.

Wesley heard the edge and instinctively recognized the timbre. When Songhai was dating Man-Man, Stokely was too young to intervene and too powerless to alter his sister's fate. As a man, he had some ability to protect his sister, and that's what colored his words. Wes understood. Having long been recognized as the cool head among Stokely's friends, Wes let all that confrontational energy bypass him and casually affirmed, "I've never been more serious in my whole life."

The men looked at each other for a moment. Stokely was looking as if searching for a clue, something not easily seen. Wesley's glance was one of opening, sort of a beckoning that said, "Look all you want, there is nothing to see but sincerity." The moment passed with Stokely smiling broadly, "I suppose we'll be brothers for real." They dapped each other and shared a man-hug. "Yep, we're real brothers."

Early December 4, 1964

Columbus figured his mother would be nearing the end of her shift at the hospital and that his brother, Cleveland, was asleep. Usually, Cleveland left the inside chain lock unfastened if Columbus had not returned before he went to bed. However, tonight or better yet, this morning was different. After keying the lock and pushing the door, Columbus' entry was halted by the chain lock. The abruptness at which the door stopped caused him to bump his face against it. In anger he shouted, "Cleve, man, what the fuck! Cleve! C'mon and open this damn door!" With that he pushed against the door several times before Cleve unfastened it.

Cleveland's body language was that of spent depletion. Columbus didn't notice, he commenced to fussing upon entering the unit. "Gotdam man, why the hell you switching it up tonight? Shit, you know how we do." Cleve sat and stared up at his brother with blank eyes. Columbus continued, "It would have been fucked up if I was stuck out there when Mama came home. She would been raising all kinda hell about me respecting her house and you know I don't want to hear none of that shit."

Cleveland bit his lip, saying nothing. Columbus began to notice. "What the fuck is wrong with you? Some broad got you all uptight?" Cleveland shook his head, "no," as a dry "Nah" escaped his throat. Instinctively, Columbus sat down on the sofa opposite his brother. He dipped his head in some unspoken effort to see into Cleveland's eyes. He saw that they were bloodshot red. "What the fuck you been drinking? If Mama catch you drinking, she gonna be all over your ass." Columbus leaned forward and sniffed as if to determine how heavily his brother had been drinking, which would have been odd given that Cleveland had a reputation for baby-sitting one can of Stroh's all night. His sniffing didn't pick up any scent of alcohol. Columbus leaned back and stated matter-of-factly, "Cleve, you my brother, and I hate to kick you while you're down, but you be falling for these broads too hard, too fast. Which one of these heifers done broke your heart now?" Cleveland nodded another, "no."

"Aw shit, you done got too sentimental. Look, I'mma catch some zzzz's before Mama gets home. I'll school you on how to deal with the ladies tomorrow." Cleveland's nod gave voice to a somberly cold declaration, "Mama ain't coming home tonight." Columbus was puzzled. "Damn, she doing a double shift to save up for Christmas?" Cleveland's mouth and lips formed the word "no," but the syllable was silent. "Then whatcha mean about Mama not coming home?"

As Cleveland looked into his brother's eyes, tears began seeping from his own. Columbus' confusion gave way to frustration before arriving at awareness. Awareness snatched the sheen of vibrant adolescent defiance from Columbus and left him with the visage of a frightened, wide-eyed boy. The last time he felt this way, he buried his face in his mother's hip to avoid looking at the dangling carcass of his father.

But Mama was not there, nor would she ever be again. Columbus' expression conveyed a question that Cleveland's closed eyelids and slow head nod confirmed. Much like the slow toppling of a tower, Columbus leaned all the way over to one side, and then, as if triggered by contact, when the side of his face met with the sofa cushion, a soul-aching sob broke free from his lungs.

That night, the brothers cried together from a shared bond of anguish, a profound fear of the unknown, and the morose acceptance of being parentless.

34

LOVE'S GONNA GET'CHA

Boogie Down Productions

April 3, 2015

Wilhelmina Thigpen was a lot of things, but verbose was not one. Perhaps it comes from a nearly half-century union with a loquacious minister. Maybe it's just her personality. Some consideration could be given to her age, which sprung from formative years spent being taught to keep her dress down and her legs and mouth shut. Who knows? But what was known was that Mother Thigpen would often remark, "If it don't getcha in de wash, it's gonna getcha in de rinse."

Her husband, Amos, was about to get rinsed.

Which, to her calculations, was long overdue. As a girl with a son fathered by a smooth-talking, rolling stone of a man, the security Wilhelmina gained from marrying Amos initially diminished her shame and provided a bit of security for her and her boy. Throughout the decades of their marriage, Amos would frequently remind her that he took her in when all others had cast her aside. He would then add how the Lord does that for his lost sheep. The gratitude she once felt transformed into resentment. A resentment that grew each time Amos shamed her boy for his effeminate ways or perverted God's word from redemption to persistent judgment.

For Wilhelmina, the final straw of Amo's gospel distortion came when he joined a handful of other pastors and staged a press conference saying how the Lord told them Detroit should have casinos. Wilhelmina was suspicious that those prominent ministers had been bought, and while she was never privy to the financial status of their home or the church, she knew that Amo's ministry was not lucrative enough to mortgage the building the church moved into months after that casino announcement. Other folks use the term "tipping point," but Wilhelmina refers to the casino endorsement as the time when Amos began venturing away from the straight and narrow path of Christ.

She was affirmed in this belief because the Lord would not condone the humiliation of a young man wrestling with his sexuality. Her God would not do that. Neither would Jesus endorse inserting oneself into every public matter possible, particularly if there is no ministry involved with all that self-promotion. Amos was aware of Wilhelmina's skepticism of his ministry and addressed it in so-called conversations detailing how the Lord directed him to get involved with the schools. Wilhelmina learned that there were corporations that backed local ministers in their bid to develop charter schools. The corporations hid in the background, and the community associated the minister with the school and assumed God's hand was involved. There were hands involved, and those hands periodically moved cash from one hand to another. None of that cash was used for tithing, either.

Now, after all these years of parading around the city talking about helping the families, even as he stabbed that principal in the back, Wilhelmina could feel that things were about to turn on Amos in a way he could not see. For a man whose self-assuredness makes him assume he is the smartest person in the room and a man who shuns the help from his browbeaten spouse, karma was about to boomerang back.

Oh yeah, it's gonna getcha in the rinse.

REVEREND THIGPEN BEGAN THE MORNING IN HIS OFFICE AT the woefully under-enrolled Ella Baker Academy. Since the departure of Principal Robeson, parents and staff have exercised their displeasure by finding other schools where they can teach and learn. In fact, only the first floor of the three-story building was being used. They turned off the lights and heating on the upper floors to save money. Nevertheless, Reverend Thigpen powered forward, casting blame and otherwise deflecting his shortcomings as a school leader.

After gathering his things in preparation for a noon meeting in the Governor's Office in Lansing, Reverend stopped at the front desk to retrieve a package that had been delivered to him. The box was heavier than it appeared. Because the contents were so well packed, shaking the box revealed no hints as to what was inside. Stupidly, he asked the secretary, "What's this?" She rolled her eyes and responded dryly, "A package for you." He missed or ignored the sarcasm and continued, "I wasn't expecting any package." To which she replied, "Maybe it's one of those mysterious ways of the Lord."

This time he rolled his eyes even as he commenced to open the box. Using his car key, he poked through the tape covering the space where the flaps meet. He anxiously removed the styrofoam and bubble wrap packaging to uncover an eighteen-inch-tall ceramic lawn jockey. The face of the lawn jockey was painted deep brown and had exaggerated African features. The jockey was mounted on a base which was engraved with an insult: "To the jackass who loves to hold Massa's mule."

Reverend recoiled in disgust and slammed the figure to the ground. As it shattered, he began stomping on the larger pieces. A first grader stood outside the office doorway, attempting to make sense of the scene. The secretary shouted with fake joy, "The spirit is moving!" Which brought Reverend back to his senses. He tugged at his suit lapel, turned toward the door, and shouted, "Have someone clean that up!" as he headed out. The student hurriedly moved aside, and Reverend stormed past without noticing him. When the student entered the office, he stood amid the ceramic shards. He bent over to retrieve the engraved plaque and walked it over to the secretary, who gave him a maternal hug while whispering, "Oh, don't mind, Reverend. He's having a bad day." The student found comfort in her embrace.

Moments later, when she had a chance to read the plaque, she chuckled aloud, "I know that's right!"

"THE GOVERNOR WILL NOT BE ABLE TO JOIN US THIS MORNING," said the stoic attorney. Seated beside her was one of the same officials who accompanied her to the meeting with Wellington Shelby. "However, we have the governor's full endorsement to carry forth his agenda."

She slid a printed agenda across the table to Reverend Thigpen, who perused it curiously.

The official stated, "Everything shared in this meeting is privy to four people." Then, without naming the four, he pointed to himself, the attorney, Reverend Thigpen, and the direction of the governor's office. "In the event that any of this information becomes public, we will know its source." An ominously pregnant silence hung in the air until Reverend nodded his head in a nonverbal gesture of agreement.

"We can proceed through this agenda rather quickly unless you have questions."

Thigpen again nodded his silent consent.

"We have confirmed with the authorizing institution that the charter for Ella Baker Academy will not be renewed. Its enrollment is a financial drain on all parties; however, they have consented to keeping it open until the end of this school year." They looked to Reverend for his understanding. He confirmed it with a nod.

"The next agenda item is closely related to the third. The Educational Acceleration Association School Reform District will cease to exist as we know it." Reverend gave his silent consent before the attorney continued, "However, its replacement will be a larger Detroit Neighborhood School District that will absorb all academic responsibilities from Detroit Public Schools. The Detroit Public School district will only exist to pay down its debts."

Reverend Thigpen swallowed a lump of pained regret.

The attorney continued, "Leadership for the Neighborhood School District will be handled by an appointee whom the governor is committed to selecting from the outside."

Reverend finally mustered a question, "The people of Detroit won't have control of their schools?"

The committee of two shook their heads "no" as one responded, "They are fiscally irresponsible, so we must take over for the good of all involved parties."

What Reverend swallowed this time would best be described as bile, yet he managed another question—"What about me?"

"The governor suggests you maintain current appearances and minimize any public speaking engagements including sermons at your church. In doing so, the governor hopes to make you the Emergency Manager of the City of Highland Park."

Thigpen recognized that he was a pawn in a game larger than himself. While his initial concerns were about himself and how he would spin things to include the Lord, a fleeting concern about the students and teachers of Detroit shot through his worries like a comet in the night. Once it passed, he resumed thinking of himself.

When the officials concluded, "We're glad we could agree on all the agenda items." The Reverend's acquiescence was comparable to Judas' kiss—an act of betrayal to the trust of Detroiters.

35

WE'RE A WINNER

The Impressions

May 12, 2015
Midtown Detroit

"Today is a special day!" Dr. Daniels announced it with her greetings. "We have mom, dad, and the beloved daughter, Songhai!" With that, Dr. Daniels rose to give Songhai a big welcome hug.

Songhai was happily at ease. Seated between her parents, she could see the value of their joining her for this first session. Cleve had joked that not only was he passing the therapy baton he received from Elaine to his daughter, but he also joked that she would not have to use any sick days for her visits. That joke eased Song's unfounded worries and the good energy persisted, causing her to smile as she looked side to side at both parents, before leaning forward with her elbows on her knees and asking, "Where should I start?"

"Honey, wherever you like," Dr. Daniels said with a warm smile.

May 26, 1987
The Robeson Home, Detroit

Songhai was inconsolable.

In her first year of actively reading the newspaper, she feverishly devoured any story related to the Detroit Pistons. Her father had even taken her to a few games at the Silverdome. Depending on the day, she would say either Isiah Thomas or Joe Dumars was her favorite player. Actually, there was a correlation between that declaration and which of their jerseys she had used as a pajama top.

The 1986-87 season was a breakthrough season for the Pistons. They were transforming from an occasional playoff team into championship contenders. Songhai and nearly all Pistons fans equated the team's championship legitimacy with their ability to best Larry Bird and the Boston Celtics.

Tonight, it looked like it was going to happen. It had been years since the Pistons won a game in the Boston Garden, and with a one-point lead with five seconds to go, it appeared that tonight would be the night that things changed.

Until it wasn't and they didn't.

Cleve watched slack-jawed.

Song let out a slowly escalating volume "Noooo-OOOOOOO!" as Larry Bird swooped in, intercepted Isiah's inbound pass, then flung it over to Celtic teammate Dennis Johnson, who laid the ball in the basket and secured the victory for the Celtics.

Songhai's scream and subsequent crying did not awaken Stokely, who was sprawled out on the couch and snoring. She had consistently chided her little brother's commitment to the Pistons, and in her eyes, his sleeping during a playoff game was proof of his fair-weather fandom.

However, it was a school night and in addition to

Elaine's disdain for Cleve allowing the children to stay up past their bedtime, Song's blood-curdling scream compelled Elaine to throw off the covers and rush to the family room. She was tying her robe as she raced down the hallway to find Cleve standing in front of the television, talking indecipherably while holding a crying ten-year old, Song, in his arms as if she were a toddler. When sports competitions became heated, Cleveland was prone to standing in front of the television and shouting instructions as if he were the coach and the players could hear him. Elaine approximated from Cleve's position that all of this emotion was related to the Pistons game. Although she hated to see her baby in pain, she found it rather endearing that Song was crying on her dad's shoulder while intermittently looking back at the television. She figured the Pistons lost a close game and that Song would be both sleepy and grouchy in the morning. Cleve would handle that. She was going to return to bed. As she turned to head back, she caught a glimpse of Stokely asleep on the couch. She found it amusing how he spent so much energy pleading to stay awake past bedtime only to fall asleep at the regular time. Yeah, these were her children, she thought amusingly as she returned to bed.

When the final buzzer sounded, the Boston fans screamed in delirious pandemonium, while the Pistons and their fans fell into varying states of shock and despair. Cleve began to rock Song side-to-side while rubbing her back. He interspersed comments to the television with consoling words for his daughter.

"That damn Larry Bird!"

"Alright now baby, it ain't over. They gotta come to the Silverdome for Game 6."

"Shit! We almost had it!"

"I know honey but real champions bounce back from

adversity. That's how you can tell champs from chumps. Champs always bounce back."

May 12, 2015
Dr. Daniels' Office

Songhai retold the story of the Pistons' loss, their subsequent championships, and how Cleve would remind her, "See, they're champs, not chumps." She shared that story as well as a frequent quote from her mother's letters to her in prison, "Delays are not denials."

She was so enraptured in the story that she didn't recognize the wet eyes of everyone else in the room. She continued to explain how she would tell herself she wasn't no chump and that the delays in her parole attempts were not denials of her eventual freedom. She went on about how she relied on those adages and her family's support as a means of making it through her time behind bars. She concluded her sharing by acknowledging her ongoing feelings of failure, disappointment, and wasted time. She was having a difficult time forgiving herself.

Then it was Cleve's turn.

He sighed deeply before sharing, "My old friend, Odell, died."

To which Song asked, "The guy with the roaches?"

Cleve chuckled, "Yeah, that's him." After looking at Song, he laughed harder. "The way you bolted from the house you would've thought there was a fire!" Their laughter caused Elaine and Dr. Daniels to share smiles.

Cleve resumed, "Yeah, me and Dell went way back, all the way to high school over at Northern." Cleve was shaking his head as he recalled a few other friends, "Anyhow, Dell, Sylvester, Ossie, Big Frank, Old Gaines; a whole lot of my friends are dying. And it makes me..." He looked around before continuing, "It makes me think of just how much time I have left." He paused even longer. "Funny, since me and Song started working together, the business is making more money. I love her as my baby and my partner. What's scary is lately, I feel without her, I couldn't even continue to do this work. I mean, she might think I'm teaching her and I am. But I'm …" his words trailed off as he looked at the ceiling. Song leaned over and rested her head on his shoulder, and he instinctively raised a hand to caress her face. Elaine looked on with concern. Cleve found the words, "It's like I'm depending on her to do the work I used to do." A little laugh escaped him when he added, "She gonna be a master plumber sooner than I was and, and..." His words trailed off.

The worry etched across Elaine's brow was a cue for Dr. Daniels to join in. "Songhai and Cleveland, I have a perspective that may have some value for you." The three patients looked to her with expectant eyes. "Perhaps it is fitting that both father and daughter share similar challenges." Father and daughter looked at each other before looking back at their therapist. "It seems to me that both of you are speculating and lamenting about what may come, while minimizing and occasionally devaluing the beauty of the present." While her statement was presented as just an observation, Dr. Daniel had hit the bullseye of truth. Elaine contained the "Amen!" she wanted to shout and simply nodded her head in agreement while pointing at her husband and daughter as if to say, "Yeah, both of y'all."

"Cleveland, I don't know Odell, Big Frank, or any of the others, but I do know that the grief that comes with losing our friends includes reminders of our own mortality. You and I know that death is a part of this journey, and all we can control is the quality of the journey. Now I ask, without any judgement of your friends, is there one whose life you would have wanted to trade places with... " Before she could finish,

Cleve answered, "Hell no. I mean, them my partners and I loved them like brothers. You know what I mean? But them dudes..." he sighed. "They made some choices I wouldn't have made."

Dr. Daniels jumped in, "Wouldn't have? Cleveland you did not make their choices. No disrespect to the deceased, I feel that you are here today because of the choices you made and are making. Cleveland, you are alive and the fact that these two lovely ladies are with you, have been with you, and will continue to be with you is because of the choices you made." Dr. Daniels reached for his hand and said, "Be fully present in this blessed life you have, Cleveland. Don't squander your todays worrying about tomorrows you can't control and yesterdays that have already passed. You can control being present. Be here now, and bask in the beauty of the life you created."

Cleveland absorbed Dr. Daniels' words and a smile began to emerge. While he had arrived at the appointment with a loathing of aging, he was now beginning to recognize the blessing that aging can be. Song held his hand and Elaine reached over to rub his thigh.

Dr. Daniels then addressed Song. "I know this is our first session, Songhai, yet much like your father, I believe your healing lies in your ability to be present. You will need to let go of who you think you should be and embrace who you are. Yes, it was fucked up how you got railroaded, but you were never, nor will you ever be a 'chump.' You survived what has broken many. Not only that, you are an active blessing to your parents and are mastering a line of work that will always be in need. You co-own a business, and according to your parents, you even have a serious love interest." Songhai blushed.

"Sistergirl, you've got it going on!" Dr. Daniels said with

excitement, while extending her hand for a high five. Both Song and Elaine reached out for high fives.

"Together, we will teach you some practices to move you beyond regret. You're already a champion; we just need you to embrace it with awareness." That pronouncement caused both Cleve and Elaine to look at their daughter with encouraging eyes. She met both of their gazes before smiling back at Dr. Daniels. She pointed at herself and asked, embarrassingly, "I'm a champion?"

Dr. Daniels responded with an empathic "Yes."

Elaine added, "And been one."

Cleve rounded it out, "Girl, you're the winner Curtis Mayfield was singing about."

Then everyone looked at Cleveland before erupting into spontaneous laughter.

Dr. Daniels stood and gestured with her hands for everyone to come together. They all stood and gathered for a group hug. They even leaned forward, touching foreheads. As they looked at each other with smiles, Dr. Daniels asked, "Cleve, you want to share a little of that Curtis Mayfield song with us?"

"Oh hell yeah!" He began terribly channeling Mayfield's falsetto as he began the lyrics to the classic song. Then he stepped out of the circle and commenced to do his little two-step choreography. When he extended his hand, it was taken by his daughter, who sang the ad-libs about moving up as she stood atop Cleve's work boots so that he could guide her steps. Elaine clasped her hands together and beamed brightly. Dr. Daniels did some two-stepping of her own.

At that moment, in the therapist's office, a daughter was fully present in a dance with her father.

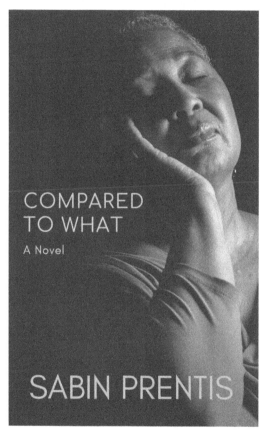

Compared To What - 2019

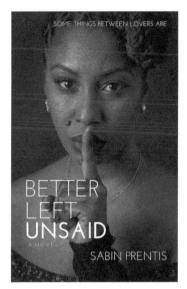

Better Left Unsaid - 2017

Leadership Pieces - 2021

Four Floors (with Ran Walker) - 2014

CDs, Records, & Tapes - 2020

Listen Up
A Memoir of Perspective

Fred Duncan with Sabin Duncan

Listen Up with Fred L. Duncan, Jr. - 2016

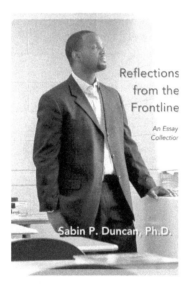

Reflections from the Frontline - 2010

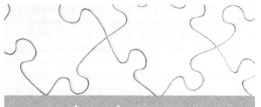

Leadership Pieces

A COMPOSITE OF VIRTUES

Sabin P. Duncan, Ph.D.

Leadership Pieces - 2021

ABOUT THE AUTHOR

Dr. Sabin Prentis Duncan is a husband, father and Creator of Literary Soul Food. He holds an Executive Masters from Georgetown University's McDonough School of Business, Doctorate and Specialist degrees from Eastern Michigan University, and Masters and Bachelor degrees from Hampton University. He writes fiction & Hip Hop essays as Sabin Prentis and non-fiction as Sabin P. Duncan.

For more information visit:
fieldingbooks.com

CPSIA information can be obtained
at www.ICGtesting.com
Printed in the USA
BVHW030833281221
624747BV00021B/23